YOUR FAULT

ANDREW COWAN was born in Corby and educated at the University of East Anglia. His first novel, *Pig*, was the winner of the *Sunday Times* Young Writer of the Year Award, a Betty Trask Award, the Ruth Hadden Memorial Prize, the Authors' Club First Novel Award and a Scottish Council Book Award, and was shortlisted for five other literary prizes. He is also the author of the writing guidebook *The Art of Writing Fiction* and four other novels: *Common Ground*, *Crustaceans*, *What I Know* and *Worthless Men*. He is the Director of the Creative Writing programme at UEA.

YOUR FAULT

ANDREW COWAN

CROMER

PUBLISHED BY SALT PUBLISHING 2019

2 4 6 8 10 9 7 5 3 1

First published in Great Britain in 2019 by
Salt Publishing Ltd
12 Norwich Road, Cromer, Norfolk NR27 0AX United Kingdom

www.saltpublishing.com

Salt Publishing Limited Reg. No. 5293401

A CIP catalogue record for this book is available from the British Library

ISBN 978 1 78463 180 2 (Paperback edition)
ISBN 978 1 78463 181 9 (Electronic edition)

Typeset in Neacademia by Salt Publishing

Printed and bound in Great Britain by Clays Ltd, Elcograf S.p.A

Salt Publishing ⸻ ⸻ .nt.
This book is made from Forest Stewardship Council™ certified paper.

For Lynne and Rose

1962

your earliest memory

THIS, THEN, IS your earliest memory.

You are no older than three because your sister is still in her pram, a Leeway 'Lugano' with chromium-plated chassis and white pneumatic wheels. The day is sunny and warm, so perhaps it is summer, which means your likeliest age is two and two thirds. Let's settle on that: August 1962. You were born on the first day of the decade, which means you are now two and two thirds.

The sky is very high and there is space all around you, hurtling away from you. It reaches your mother, who is striding into the distance in her strappy high heels, pushing your sister in her blue canvas stroller. The sun sparks in the chromium. Her heels clip on the pavement.

At this age your mother is Mummy, and Mummy is taking you somewhere, you would not know where. In fact, she has no choice but to take you – both you and your sister – since she is a housewife and mother. She can leave the house whenever she wants to – no one is stopping her; it isn't a prison – but she cannot stop being your mother. Perhaps that is why she is so cross.

You are not being taken on a trip, then. It is not for your sake that she is taking you with her. You are old enough to understand this. Your future self, looking back at yourself, will decide that you are old enough to understand this, aged two years and eight months.

You are coming towards the end of your long curving street. You have already followed your mother around the last bend, which means your house is now lost to you. Should you dare to look back you would not be able to see it. But you do not dare to look back, because then you would lose sight of Mummy, who is striding away from you, as though to escape from you.

She cannot escape you.

The concrete pavement between you and Mummy is grey, a grey so pale it is almost white. The road beside you is a different grey, a grey so dark it is almost black. There are no motor cars to be seen, but on the far side of the junction there is a row of Corporation-let garages, six alternately-coloured metal doors beneath a low corrugated roof. The sequence runs *red, blue and green; red, blue and green.* Throughout your estate you will find other such patterns, for instance in the doors of the houses to your left, which are set back twenty feet from the road and fronted by freshly mown lawns. The sequence of these doors runs *mustard and blue; mustard and blue; mustard and blue.*

The open-plan lawns belong to the Corporation, and are mown by the Corporation. The tenants are required to trim the edges with shears or clippers, and are encouraged to plant flowers appropriate to the seasons, but they are not permitted to alter the style or colour of their doors. The sycamore tree that towers over the garages has been left there to provide scenic interest, vegetative variety in the built environment. It terminates the prospect. The curvilinear road layout is intended to obviate the impression of monotony. Naturally you won't know this, or even know that you don't yet know it. The tenant's handbook will help you, years later. Also the internet, books.

This is your earliest memory and it has no end or beginning, no afterwards and before. You are stranded in this moment, snatched from an immediate past you did not wish to be snatched from, and led towards a future you do not wish to be led to. Such is a life. Your mother has quickened her stride to get away from you, to make you feel left behind, and you have refused to hurry after her. Instead you have come to a halt on the white pavement, beneath this blue summer sky, and you are bawling, abandoned and furious. You stamp your sandalled feet, and when Mummy stops at the junction and turns and angrily shouts for you to come along *now*, you do not come along.

Peter! she shouts. *I am warning you!*

Your name, then, is Peter – let's settle on that – and Mummy is becoming impatient. Time is now pressing.

And the next thing: there is nothing but the inevitability that she will come back and you will be spanked. This much you understand. But you have no resources. You do not want to keep walking, to go where they are going – your sister and Mummy – but neither do you wish to be abandoned, left alone on this pavement, and so you stamp your feet and refuse.

You bawl at your mother and wait for your future to reach you, a future you do not want but cannot prevent. This may be your inciting incident, the point at which your story begins. For now, let us suppose so. Here comes fury. Here comes a spanking.

Many times you will come back here; you may not want to but you will. Many times you will remember this moment, these pavements, these lawns, your mother striding towards you, her fury, and when finally you reach your father's age – the age at which he died – you will remember it all, as much as there is, as much as you are able to.

Obviously you cannot yet know this. Unwittingly, as you stand and stamp your sandalled feet, you are anticipating your future recollection of this moment, when all of this will have happened, which will cause you to recall another such moment, another tantrum, in which your sister's stroller is parked outside the Fine Fare and the pavement is damp, dully gleaming in the murk of November; probably November, still in 1962. You are in the shopping precinct and you have flopped to the pavement beside the Spastics Society girl and you are refusing to cooperate; you will not do as Mummy tells you to do.

At this age, the Spastics Society girl is taller than you are. All through your childhood she will stand outside the supermarket. She is cast in metal and flatly resounds if you strike her. She has blond hair and a short blue dress and a brown metal teddy tucked under her right arm. She wears a caliper on her right leg and stands on a heavy black plinth that means you need help to reach the slot in her collection box: PLEASE HELP YOUR LOCAL SPASTICS.

Perhaps Mummy has grown tired of lifting you up; perhaps she has no more coppers to spare. It is not a toy, she will say in her accent, as if repeating a line from a phrasebook. Money does not grow on trees, she will add, and refuse to let you drop any more coins in the slot. Whatever the reason, you are once again bawling, only this time Mummy is holding your arm, gripping your wrist through your winter coat as she attempts to yank you upright so that she can once again spank you.

Of course you try to evade her, but you cannot escape, just as she cannot escape you, or land a clean blow, and you sense her frustration, also her embarrassment. The shopping precinct is busy, and even in the midst of your misery, as you writhe about on the damp pavement, becoming clammy with refusal, you notice the passers-by and recognize their disapproval, whether of you or your mother you never will know, not even in recollection.

Possibly they disapprove of your mother because of her accent, her foreign complexion. There is that; there will always be that. But if they were to follow your mother and her two children home, these strangers, might they also disapprove of the readiness with which she loses her temper, or the persistence with which you test it, forever trying her patience? Might they suspect you of seeking her anger because you enjoy the tussle that follows, her ineffectual slaps hitting your thighs as she attempts to find your bottom and you refuse to allow her? Do you sometimes laugh? In your recollection you will sometimes laugh, and so will she. But sometimes too her exasperation will bring her to tears, and her grip will tighten on your arm and she will hurt you.

Stop, you're hurting me! you will complain.

Then stand *still!* she will scream at you. Peter, stand *still!* You are making me *mad!*

Your father's anger is colder, and his blows are much harder, more sudden. But he isn't your real father, you will come to believe. That must be why.

Even at two years and eight months there is much that is lost to you, already forgotten, if indeed it was ever known to you. Most of your life to this point might never have happened.

At one time, for instance, you too were a baby, just as your sister is now. There is a Kodacolor booklet of photographs to prove this. The cover of the booklet is primrose yellow, and each of its stiff pages has four perforations, curved like thumbnails, one slit in each corner. The photographs tuck into the slits. For now, these slits are as interesting to you as anything contained in the photographs, which present a bland little baby in a white lacy gown.

In some of the photos the baby appears in your mother's arms. She wears a pair of horn-rimmed spectacles and a red cardigan, which suits her colouring, everyone says so. The glasses make her seem older. In another of the photos the baby rests in the crook of your father's left arm. He has a cigarette in his right hand – it will be an Embassy Tipped – and the knot in his tie is tugged loose. There is grey at his temples already. But in most of the photos the baby is alone, propped against the living room cushions, or laid on its back. Evidently, you are this baby. It is a boy.

Congratulations.

There are other photographs of yourself as a small child, two dozen or so, which will surprise you by revealing an image of yourself as you have never known yourself: sweetly wide-eyed and cheerful, eager and trusting. But after the birth of your sister, it seems, a great change comes about: your gaze betrays glumness, calculation, awareness. Your older self, poring over these pictures, will see this and wish that it were otherwise. Your sister may wish it were otherwise, too.

You did not ask for a sister.

For much of your childhood a favourite family story will describe the moment your father emerged from the telephone kiosk across the road from the Fine Fare, having just called the maternity hospital and received the news of her arrival. You have a baby sister, he announced, crouching down. Are you going to help Mummy look after her?

No, you said. I don't want a baby sister. I want a bunny rabbit or a baa lamb or a woof woof.

Several times over several years you will hear this story, and you will adopt it as a story that you yourself tell, since it allows you to reveal your true feelings towards your sister in a way that is more endearing than shaming. But not only will you have no memory of having said such a thing, or of your father delivering the news of her birth, in time you will come to doubt the truth of the story. A *woof woof*? Would you ever have said such a thing? Was there ever a time in your life when you would have used such an expression?

There was.

But then, it isn't always necessary to remember an event or a period in your life for its after-effects to be felt. The details may be lost to you, but that time before your sister's arrival, those two and a half years of being the only child – your mother's sole treasure – have survived and will continue to survive as the absence of something, a lack you may never identify, a loss you may never make good; another one.

1963

It is Daddy; watch out!

THE ESTATE WHERE you live is for children and mums. The dads must go off to work, and most of them work in the Works, your own father included. Let us call him your father. Daily he leaves his family behind, sometimes before you have woken, sometimes after your bedtime, and often his absence will not be noticed until he returns, bringing with him the stench of the Works – that stale male industrial smell of sweat and grease and machines – into the home you share with your mother and sister, which is fragranced with Pledge and Persil and Palmolive soap, your mother's perfume, her cooking.

Of course your father will sometimes be home – sleeping after a night shift, smoking after a day shift, getting ready to leave for his back shift – and usually you will know he is there in a way that is never the case with your mother, whose constant presence is taken for granted. If Mummy is away you will feel it; if Daddy is at home you will feel it. This is one difference between them, and is in the nature of things, at least until you learn that Mummy cannot be relied on, that she too can abandon you – for hours, even days at a time.

This may be the earliest instance: she says she will not be gone long, you must stay in the living room and play. You must not play in the kitchen, do you hear me? Peter, do you hear me? You must not go upstairs either, not unless you need to go to the toilet. Do you need to go to the toilet? Your sister is having her afternoon nap. You must be a good boy and try not to wake her.

And your reward for being a good boy? Mummy allows you to play with your sister's collection of toys, which your father forbids you from touching. She lifts out the cardboard box from under the sideboard, and a little while later the back door clicks shut. If a key turns in the lock you do not hear it. You are kneeling on the carpet, emptying the box of its toys.

You have not yet started in school: that remains in your future. You are now three and a half, at an age when the backs of the settee and the chairs are still some way above the height of your head. The furniture is the same age as the house, which means it is the same age as yourself: a matching settee and two armchairs from the Sarno *New Idea* Collection, bought on hire purchase from the Co-operative Department Store, which is next to the bus station in the town centre.

You do not yet know these things.

The backs of the chairs and the arms of the settee provide landing stages for your sister's toys as you fly them in your hands through the air, from one chair-back and arm-rest to another.

Softly you hum as they fly. This is what you do in the moments after Mummy leaves you, when you play nicely with your sister's toys in the living room on your own.

There is Looby Loo and a Rosebud Sleeping Doll that resembles a baby, with black nylon hair and hard plastic eyelids that close when she is tilted. It does not matter that she is a doll. Boys can play with dolls too if they want to. You give the toys voices, and they speak to each other quietly, nicely, as they leap from chair-back to chair-back then pause to look around.

Where is Mummy? asks the doll.

She won't be gone long, says Looby.

Where is Daddy?

He is at work.

You lay the doll on its back, and she closes her eyes. You lay Looby beside her, and her eyes do not close. Then you return to the other toys on the floor and choose a small wiry teddy with articulated shoulders and hips, and a floppy knitted kitten called Flopsy, whose eyes are black buttons. You sit them side by side on the arm of the settee, but a monster is coming and they must get away, go quickly, go now.

It is Daddy; watch out!

The teddy and Flopsy make aeroplane noises as they take off, and noises like missiles as they descend. They collide with the chair-back and explode. You let go of them, and watch as they tumble to the carpet. The teddy lands face down, his legs and arms stiff. One of Flopsy's legs is folded beneath her. You sweep Looby Loo to the carpet as well, where she too explodes, then you propel the doll after her.

You crouch down beside them. You take the dolls and the teddy in your hands and bring them crashing together. You grind them into each other. But you are not hurting them; they are hurting each other and they must stop it. You tell them to stop it at once – do you hear me? – and throw them apart. They are making you *mad*.

You shake the knitted kitten and Looby Loo so their heads flop wildly back and forth. Then you bite Looby's shoulder. You clamp the padded fabric hard in your mouth and feel the meeting of your milk teeth through the padding. She has not been a good girl. She is a bad girl. You bite harder, as hard as you can, until you feel the pain that she must be feeling, then you discard Looby Loo and climb onto the chair that is nearest the front window.

You stand on the chair-arm, high up in the air, dangerously high – Peter, get down from there! – and stare into the street through the white Venetian blinds. You are crying. The street is empty. Daddy is at work; Mummy has gone. Your sister is sleeping, and you are alone.

Your town is a new town, designed for the future, and the Bawdeswell estate is the newest part of the new town. In fact, it is barely older than you are, and has no history, no memory. You will hear this said many times, until it becomes part of the history of the town, a thing that people remember about it.

You live at number 78 Bawdeswell Avenue, in the house where you were born, upstairs in Mummy and Daddy's bedroom. The house is spacious and semi-detached, and as familiar to you as your parents' faces, or the sound of their voices.

On the other side of the wall live Peggy and Bill, whose grown-up sons have already left home. Sometimes you hear them: Peggy's screechy complaints, Bill's grumbling replies. And no doubt they can hear you. Peggy hears you crying now, for instance – both you and your sister. Your cries for Mummy have disturbed your sister's afternoon nap, and they have disturbed Peggy, too. She has come outside to see what is the matter. She is standing in the middle of the front lawn.

On your estate there are fourteen houses to the acre, and on Bawdeswell Avenue the houses are laid out so that none must confront another square-on. No housewife need open her curtains to find a neighbour staring straight back in at her. The street is arranged so that neighbourliness is encouraged and privacy respected. Short terraces of four and six houses are oriented at a thirty degree angle to the road; others are grouped around irregular lawns, grassy knolls. Rows of semi-detacheds progress in echelon fashion, each frontage recessed from its neighbour. Modest blocks of flats are surrounded by shrubberies and tidy greens in which are planted saplings. There is unity and variety. In scale and style, the houses are not unalike, but there is diversity too. Some have pebble-dash rendering, others timber boarding, and many are clad in hanging tiles, slate-grey or terracotta. Your tiles are slate-grey.

How many thousands of times will you look out on this scene? How many thousands of times will it return to you?

The pavement in front of your house is three and a half slabs wide to the kerb, a distance of six feet. The road is sixteen feet wide, and curves directly opposite your house into a side-street that climbs a short incline, then opens out to a playing field. The field is called Seething Green, and it seems to you as a child to be vast. Lengthily it descends to a swing park, beyond which begins another incline, and another snaking avenue, leading to the shopping precinct: the Lingwood Road shops.

From the vantage of your chair-arm you can see the flat-roofed flats above the shops that mark your furthest horizon, a quarter of a mile in the distance. Mummy must have gone to the shops; this is what you believe. And here in her absence is Peggy, angling to see into your house.

No hedge or rail encloses the lawn. Nothing distinguishes your side of the grass from next-door's, but Peggy is poised as though there were a dividing line, over which she must not step. She wears a floral pinarette and matching headscarf in yellow and green, white 'shortie' jeans and white leather casuals, and she is leaning across to her left, almost on tiptoes, straining to see into your living room. Her painted-on eyebrows are raised as if in surprise.

Of course she would not be standing on the lawn if Mummy were here. You realise this, and the realisation makes you cry louder because you have been abandoned. You cry so loudly you fail to hear the back door, your mother returning.

She hurries into the living room. Hush, hush, she says, and lifts you away from the chair-arm, hoiks you onto her hip. Why are you crying? You are a big boy, you should not be crying like this. She is annoyed, but she is Mummy. You wrap your arms around her neck as she carries you across to the window. Look at poor Peggy, she says; you have made her so worried.

Slyly you look out at poor Peggy, who is still standing on the lawn. Mummy nuzzles the top of your head and waves through the blinds and Peggy waves back, a cigarette between two of her fingers. Upstairs your sister continues to cry but Peggy is no longer so worried. She returns to her own house and your mother sighs and puts you down, because you are so heavy, such a very big boy. She does not say where she has been, and you do not ask her: she cannot have gone far.

Your older self, looking back, will come to certain conclusions, but for now, Mummy has not gone away, and all will be well. She goes upstairs to attend to your sister, and you kneel on the carpet, your sister's toys strewn around you. You select a small plastic doll. You wrench its arms from their sockets.

Ever since your sister was born you have been told that you are a big boy. At three and a half you are already a big boy, and you understand that you are to feel proud of this. But still you cannot help wishing that your sister might die or be returned to the hospital or given away so that you can go back to being your mother's sole treasure.

A great deal is expected of you. A big boy must not cry, and ought to eat all his food, and help to look after his sister, and know when he needs to go to the toilet, then take himself there, and remember to flush the toilet and wash his hands afterwards. But sometimes you do not realize in time that you need to go to the toilet. The first indication might be the sensation of dampness and warmth, then the dark spreading stain on your crotch and the inside of your thighs. What you should have anticipated has already occurred. Your body, which belongs to you but also to Mummy, has caused an accident to happen.

Mummy calls them accidents, even when she is cross with you.

Here is an example: you are kneeling on the carpet at the foot of your bed, playing alone in your bedroom with your clip-to-gether fort, which is manned by six polythene knights and two bowmen and has four crenelated towers and a fully function-ing drawbridge, portcullis and flagstaff. The flag of St George is flying, always flying, and the fort is being assailed by seven American soldiers in a variety of operational postures, one of them carrying a bazooka. That one is Daddy. Perhaps he will die. In your games, your father does often die.

The wetness spreads quickly, darkening your blue rayon shorts. They are probably rayon.

At once you abandon the game you are playing – you have already forgotten it – and descend the staircase to the living room, where Mummy is seated on the settee with a friend, another woman, whose round face is familiar, though she is not one of your neighbours. At this time it is rare for your house to have visitors, but this woman has been here before, and you sense that you like her. Their postures mirror each other, their knees looming so large beneath the taut hem of their skirts, their legs identically crossed at the ankle, cups of coffee balanced on the saucers in their laps.

They turn their heads to look at you, smiling. They are both wearing lipstick – coral pink, poppy red – and white pointy shoes with high heels. You ought not to let Mummy see you, but you do not know what else you should do. It is a conundrum, and your only solution is to parade stiffly past her, but not to admit to what has occurred.

I'm being a soldier, you announce, like my daddy.

Oh are you? says Mummy, I see; and watches as you march into the kitchen, your legs and arms straight, your shorts chafing where they have soaked through to your thighs.

In the kitchen you are surrounded by yellow, everything yellow: curtains, cupboards and drawers, two vinyl-covered stools, two vinyl-backed chairs, a table laminated in 'wonderful Warerite'. This is the Sixties.

The back door is open. Birds are calling. From here you might go out to play in the garden, despite your sodden underpants and shorts, which will in time become dry, and will not smell. Or you might hide your wet clothes in the shed – the utility room that is known in your house as 'the shed' – and select some other clothes from the pile of ironing that sits beneath the boxed-in slope of the staircase. Or you might continue to be a soldier and make the return journey past your mother and her friend on the settee and climb back up to your bedroom.

Unable to decide, you remain in the kitchen, surrounded by yellow, your head inclined to the living room, waiting for Mummy, who will surely know what to do with you.

And then she is there, kneeling on the linoleum and gripping your arm. She turns you around. Come on, she sighs, let me get you out of these clothes.

You dare not complain about the tightness of her grip. There has been an accident, for which you are to blame. But when her friend appears in the doorway, still smiling, still holding her saucer and cup, you attempt to twist the other way. Her face may be familiar, and friendly, but she must not be allowed to look at your peter, this woman who is not your mother, not even a neighbour.

He is so grown! she marvels.

Stand *still*, snaps your mother, and peels down your underpants, revealing your peter. Then: Yes, she says; yes, he is becoming a big boy.

Your penis is called your 'peter', and if ever you dwell on this fact you will suppose that everyone's private parts must be named after the person who owns them. Your father must have a 'joe'. If your mother has anything, it must be known as her 'dolores', perhaps even her 'dolly'.

Naturally your peter is smaller and softer than your father's joe, which you will see many times as he hurries from the bedroom to the toilet, or lies soaking in the bath, or wanders out from the bathroom, still towelling himself dry, his dyed wavy hair all tousled, awry.

Daddy's joe is large and meaty, a thick dangling tube, and his body is pelted all over in hair, including his shoulders and back, his fat tummy and thighs, the tops of his arms. He has sideburns too, and always a shadow of stubble. Sometimes he will shave twice in one day.

These are two of the things that distinguish him from your mother, his private parts and his hair, while a third is the stench that remains after he has taken his newspaper – his *Daily Mirror*, his *People*, his *Pink'Un* – into the toilet, where he will close the door and fasten the bolt, which you must not do. Peter, are you listening? The bolt will slide across, and for a long time then your father will remain concealed behind the door, so long you might forget that he is in there.

You must not forget that he is in there.

Time will pass, and always afterwards there will be a cigarette stub left floating in the bowl, seeping a yellowish stain from the filter, and though the stink is partly the cigarette – the acrid smell of damp ash and the taint of the smoke – mainly it is excrement, the sharp fetid reek of his poo, which is so different from the creamier, sweeter smell that lingers after your mother has been.

Mums and dads have different smells, and mums must also sit down to wee, as you have seen, since your mother does not bolt the door, or even close it. She does not like to be shut in. She does not live in a prison.

You are aware of these things, aged three and a half, and often when you wake in the morning you will listen as Mummy goes to the toilet – the clatter as the seat drops, the thunderous cascade into the bowl, the rattle of the toilet roll, the flush and the surge in the pipes – then quickly you will slip out from under your sheets and hurry in after her, releasing your peter from your pyjamas. Look at me, you will say, and stand at the bowl, aiming into the water.

Very good, she will reply; but watch what you are doing.

Another difference between them: your father will keep the bath an hour or more, and leave the towels about the floor, despite the instructions on the plaque on the wall, which you believe you can read, since Mummy has intoned them so often.

Please remember, don't forget, never leave the bathroom wet.

Peter? Can you say it?

Nor leave the soap still in the water, that's a thing we never ought'er.

Daddy's bathwater is deeper and greener than Mummy's, and much hotter, less clouded with suds. You must not put your hand in, or it will scald you. Peter, are you listening? It will burn you, says Mummy.

But at the Works Recreation Club, where Daddy takes you sometimes on Saturdays, you will be allowed to crouch beside the gargantuan taps of the men's communal baths and watch as the searing hot water surges onto the white tiles, the noise cacophonous, the steam damply warming your face. If you look over your shoulder you will find him, folding the towels. He will still have his eye on you; don't you worry about that.

Perhaps he takes you to the club to allow your mother some respite from you. Perhaps he derives some pleasure from being in your company, aged three and three quarters. Your older self, considering this, may never be sure. But these are happy excursions. At the Works Recreation Club your father is cheerful, more cheerful than you will ever see him at home. Sometimes he laughs.

It is his job at the Club to inflate the brown leather footballs for the Works' first eleven before they get changed, then make their half-time tea in two giant tea-pots, and slice some oranges into quarters, and fill the baths before the men clatter back in from the cold, spattered all over in mud and smelling sourly of grass and sweat and embrocation.

You are too young to distinguish one man's face from another; only your neighbours have faces you recognise. But these men also have peters, or joes, and in the vaporous, echoing chamber of the bathroom you will look at their joes as they sink into the green-tinted water, then retreat behind your father's legs and watch as he jokes with them, these men who are his friends; he calls them his pals.

How's that young wife of yours? they will ask him. Keeping you busy? Keeping you up nights?

They are his pals, and at one time he would have played football with them; he would have sat here in this bath full of men. That was before he injured his knee. He had to go to a hospital, where he had to have an operation. His leg was in plaster. Poor Daddy. It happened when you were a baby, before your earliest memory, and you are sorry not to have seen it, your father on crutches, in pain.

Mummy's pal is called Nadia and she does not have any children, not yet. Nor is she married. Like Mummy, she used to live far away, in a different country, though not the same one, not an island surrounded by the sea. She tells you these things as she kneels in front of you, her hands holding yours. Later you will remember staring at the gap between her front teeth, the silver cross at her throat. You will remember her dancing.

There is a wireless set, leatherette-covered in black and pink, which sits on a glass side-table in your living room. The table has a scalloped edge trimmed in gilt and ruby red, and fits into the recess to the left of the chimney breast. Beneath it lies Mummy's wicker basket of numbered knitting needles, which are not toys and not for playing with. Peter, do you hear me?

Aligned at an angle to the table is an armchair, which is not for climbing on, and not for jumping on. But you are bouncing up and down on the seat cushion, and Nadia is holding your hand to keep you from falling. She makes swivelling movements on the balls of her stockinged feet, dancing along to the Yeah Yeahs, which is your name for the Beatles. They are singing *She Loves You*. It is the autumn of 1963, probably the autumn. It could not be any earlier.

The wireless has push-button controls for selecting the wave-band and setting the tone, and two notched perspex dials for tuning and volume. Nadia has turned up the volume, and she is laughing because you are joining in with the chorus, yelling *yeah yeah yeah!* as you bounce up and down on the armchair. You are gleeful. You may be over-excited. When the Yeah Yeahs sing *oooooooooh!* Nadia sings with them, and shakes her head, which you find very funny. Her dark lacquered hair is becoming dishevelled.

Nadia's dress on this occasion has a wide pleated skirt which tucks and swirls as she turns, and in her free hand she is holding a cigarette. She inhales, and drops the cigarette into your father's ashtray on the mantelpiece, then exhales to the ceiling.

You have forgotten your father; you ought not to have forgotten him.

Anxious, still bouncing, you look around for your mother and find her standing by the kitchen. She is cradling your sister – who is wearing a bib, her face smeared orange with food – and she appears to be swaying, quietly dancing. Mummy likes to listen to music. Daddy does not.

And the next thing: the door from the hallway swings open. It slams into the wall and your father comes into the room. He has been woken from his sleep and he is naked. Your father often sleeps naked. With one hand cupped over his joe he attempts to turn off the radio, but turns the wrong dial. Static replaces the end of the Yeah Yeahs, and then there are voices. Impatient, he picks up the set and angles it towards the light from the window, his penis uncovered, now fully revealed. He turns off the wireless, and tosses it across to the empty settee, and glowers at Nadia. Get him off the fucking furniture, he says, then goes back upstairs, slamming the door after him.

You saw his bottom, too.

There is silence. You hear his footsteps on the ceiling, the creak of the bed. Nadia's face is flushed. She looks at your mother, then lets out a yelp of a laugh. Daddy has told her off, but you know that you are also to blame. And now there has been another accident. The dampness is sudden, the warmth is familiar. Quickly you climb down from the chair and run to your mother. You wrap your arms around her legs and press your face to her thigh. Her pinny smells of outdoors, as if she has just come in from the garden. She touches your head. She hasn't yet noticed.

He is on night shift, she says.

My father also, says Nadia.

It is okay. He must wake up anyway. It is almost time.

I think I must go now.

Yes, I am sorry.

Your mother is twenty-two years old. Nadia is younger. And your father, who was once a soldier, is many years older than either of them –twice as old as your mother, old enough to be her father too – which means they must do as he tells them to. Everyone must do as he tells them to.

1964

you could be anyone

IN THE CLUTCH of photographs that survive from the time that precedes you, there are so few of your father in uniform. Your favourite shows him at forty-one years old. He has achieved this age before you have yet begun. Your future self, contemplating your father, will often conjure this man, forever a soldier, squinting into the sunshine, unable to see you.

The photograph is small and monochrome and creased across its middle. It presents him dressed in khaki drill: a pale shirt and shorts, knee-high ribbed socks, beetle-black shoes and soft cap. Three stripes. And there is another just like it, similarly creased, showing your mother. The backdrop is the same: a sunlit wall, a cypress tree, a harbour behind her. But she is a girl, soon to be seventeen, with thick unruly hair and thick eyebrows. The date is written on the reverse: *June '58*. Her dress is sleeveless and collared, with a narrow belted waistline and a wide pleated skirt that reaches down to her shins. She is wearing white socks and strappy sandals. The socks are called bobby socks. Your future self, contemplating your mother, will often picture this girl.

At four years old, few of the facts are known to you. At this age you do not yet know that your parents met on the island of Malta, a British colony, where your father saw out his final few years in the army. He was a Royal Engineer, a sapper, a sergeant, who served all through the Second World War. Aged twenty-one, he was conscripted into the catering corps, having first completed his apprenticeship as a fitter in a factory in Scotland. Being in the catering corps does not mean he can cook. His time with the caterers will not last long, though he will find that soldiering suits him. He will remain for twenty more years – a regular – and once his term in Malta is over he will return not to Scotland but to your new town in England, where he will start work in the Works, earning thirteen pounds and ten shillings a week.

He will return with your mother, his wife.

As a legal minor, not yet eighteen, she will require the consent of her father, a widower, a shopkeeper, a churchgoing Catholic. An army chaplain will conduct the ceremony at Mtarfa barracks in Malta. Only one of your mother's four older sisters will be there, and none of her brothers. Your father's mother, a widow, a churchgoing Presbyterian, will not attend either.

The Maltese government will assist your mother's passage to England. It will assist the passage of four thousand others that year, to Britain and elsewhere.

There will be more to it than this, and the dates will bear

further scrutiny. But for now you are content in the knowledge that Daddy was once a soldier, and that Mummy came from far away, and that their lives before you arrived were lived in black and white.

After your birth there comes colour, the buttery shades of the Sixties, a new beginning to things.

But how much there is to remember.

The sequence of doors in your stretch of the street runs *burgundy and green; burgundy and green; burgundy and green.* Your front door is a green one. The concrete canopy over the porch is supported by a metal pole, and to the right of the door are two panes of glass, one above the other. The glass is bubbled. Coloured shapes move behind it.

Peggy and Bill's house is the same, but the other way round. Their door is burgundy, with the glass to the left, the pole to the right. Their house is number 80, and in time you will sneak into their garden and cup your hands to their windows, perturbed by the sameness, but also the differences. Sometimes you will peer through their letter box at the Toby jugs on their staircase, red-cheeked and chortling, two fat men on each step. You should not be looking. Peter, come away from there now.

The front door of your house opens into the hallway and the foot of the staircase. Another door – turn right – leads into the living room, which is as long as the house. The window at the back of the house is the same size as the window facing into the street. With the blinds fully open someone taller than you could see straight through from the street to your garden. They could wave to Mummy as she pegs out the washing. Smiling, Mummy could wave back at them.

The sun would be shining.

The living room leads into the kitchen – turn left past the fireplace – and the kitchen leads into the shed – turn left at the fridge – which is where the back door is to be found. The back door is at the side of your house and faces across to the Coatleys', who live at number 76. There's a narrow gap in the fence. Mummy could slip through it quite easily, if ever she needed to call on Ken Coatley.

She often needs to call on Ken Coatley.

Your house has a modern, straightforward appearance. The lines are clean, the surfaces plain. None of the doors, interior or exterior, is panelled and beaded. Six identical doors – Peter, can you count them? – lead off the landing at the top of the staircase: three bedrooms, a bathroom, a toilet, an airing cupboard. It disturbs you when all of these doors are closed; their blankness is troubling.

Each of the bedrooms contains a suite of matching furniture, a different suite in each room, all of it new and bought on hire purchase or with the help of the Provident. Ken Coatley works for the Provident. He calls from house to house, arranging terms, collecting repayments. He is known as the Provy Man. He is also known as a ladies man, though you would not know this, or yet know what it means.

Your sister sleeps in a cot in the smallest of the rooms, just above your front door. Her room has two matching items of furniture. Your room has three. In addition to your bed, your room contains a white wicker chair and a suite comprising a wardrobe, a dressing table, a chest of five drawers. The veneer is mahogany, so glossy and dark it reflects you, the ghostly impression of you.

In the dressing table you will find your clothes, only yours, but the chest and the wardrobe belong to your father and are not to be messed with. Peter, are you listening? They are private.

Most nights when your father is home he will come into your bedroom, the light from the landing illuminating the curls of blue smoke from his cigarette. Always he will be smoking a cigarette, which he will place on the edge of the chest and allow to burn down, become a fragile column of ash, as he changes into or out of his clothes. Mummy will not allow him an ashtray upstairs, though this won't deter him. He will tap his ash wherever he can, including her pot-plants, his teacup, the palm of his hand.

You will watch him as he undresses, the meticulousness with which he folds his jumpers, trousers and shirts, and should he see that you are awake he will come and tuck your bedclothes more tightly around you, folding the corners as neatly as his clothes, just as he was taught to in the army.

It is comforting, the tightness of the enclosure; so too his insistence that your arms should be inside the covers, your chin on the outside.

N'night, pal, he will say then, the warmest of his endearments.

Don't forget your cigarette, you might say.

I won't, he'll reply, and retrieve it from the rim of the chest as he leaves.

The door will remain ajar to the landing, at least until you are asleep, should you be able to sleep. But sometimes he will forget about his cigarette, since you are not always awake and cannot always remind him. Then it will burn back to the stub, leaving a scorch mark in the wood. There is already a row of black grooves along the rim of the chest, and one afternoon your mother discovers a new one. She is upstairs, doing the dusting. Your father is changing for his back shift.

You will set the house on fire! she screams at him. The boy will burn in his bed!

You hear this as you sit cross-legged on the tufted rug in front of the fireplace, looking up at *The Woodentops*. Your sister is sitting nearby, playing with her coloured bricks, which used to be yours.

The television is rented from B.T.S. Radio in the town centre, a Ferguson 17-inch in a polished walnut laminate cabinet, and if *The Woodentops* is showing it must be a Friday. Your favourites are *Flower Pot Men*, which airs on a Wednesday, and *Andy Pandy*, which you watch on a Tuesday. Of course, you haven't yet learned the days of the week.

The Woodentops have a larger family than yours. There is Mummy Woodentop and the baby, then Daddy Woodentop, and Willy and Jenny the twins. There is also Mrs Scrubbit, who comes to help Mummy Woodentop, and Sam who helps Daddy Woodentop, and the very biggest spotty dog you ever did see. Spotty waves with his ears. Mummy Woodentop is busy with housework. Spotty and the children walk as if they are dancing.

No nostalgia attaches to this, to any of this.

There is a scuffle, a slap, another slap, then Daddy shouting, followed by the noise of his footsteps coming down the stairs. The front door opens and slams; the Venetian blinds ripple. Upstairs your mother is crying; she is wailing. But Mummy cries often, and you remain where you are, sitting with your sister in front of the television. The bricks are wooden and make clacking noises. They stack inside a tray with red metal wheels and a blue metal push-bar. *Tri-ang* is printed on the side. Mummy did not call you *Peter*, or *your son*. She called you *the boy*. You may be absorbed in *The Woodentops*, but this is surely not lost on you. Your older self, recalling this scene, will decide that nothing here should be lost on you. You are *the boy*. It means you could be anyone. And the next thing: it seems you have struck your sister with one of the bricks, and now she too is crying; she is wailing, and you know you ought not to have done this.

For her birthday, or perhaps to make amends to her, your father buys Mummy a Fidelity radiogram. Equipped with separate treble and bass controls, push-button wave selection, and a record-changer capable of playing ten records in all sizes, at each of four speeds, the radiogram is placed in the far corner of the living room. The wood-veneer cabinet matches the television and stands on angled, ebonied legs that match the settee and chairs. The volume is ample. It boasts excellent tone.

In the stowage compartment for discs your father deposits his meagre collection of records, which he has brought downstairs from the attic. Until now, you have not been aware of the attic. He stood on a chair and hauled himself up and disappeared through a hatch in the ceiling. Be careful, called Mummy. He entered the attic, and the attic entered your imagination. One day, you decide, you too will disappear through this hatch in the ceiling. It is high up, but you are not afraid of high places, and neither is Daddy.

His record collection comprises Count Basie, Dean Martin, Frank Sinatra, Ted Heath and his Music, Jack Parnell and his Orchestra. It seems your father is attached to the styles and stars of an earlier era – the rat pack, the big band sound – having failed to catch on to Elvis, far less the Beatles. Mummy likes the Beatles, of course, and Herman's Hermits, the Tremeloes, Cliff Richard, all of those. Mummy likes new things, Daddy does not. But she will have to listen to her favourites on the radio, because she cannot afford to buy any records.

She is smiling as she says this, admiring the radiogram, and your father laughs, his big hand shaped to her bottom. Mummy is wearing red trousers. Slacks; on a lady they are called slacks.

Christmas, he says, squeezing her bottom. I'll get you some records then. How about Shirley Bassey?

Still smiling, Mummy pushes him away with her hip. It is a joke that they share. Mummy reminds him of Shirley Bassey, another of his favourites: not just her duskiness, also her temper. She is fiery, he says.

You press yourself between them, embracing one of Mummy's legs, inhaling her perfume, and sulkily stare at the radiogram. You do not like to see him touching her.

Mummy does not like you hanging on to her.

Peter, let go now, she sighs.

Years later, as you examine your father in the photographs, the nicotine stains on his fingers will become very clear to you; so too will the bruises under his nails.

In some of the photos he is dressed in his best clothes – a blazing white shirt, a tie with a tie-pin, a made-to-measure suit – yet still pinching a cigarette between his forefinger and thumb. Given the occasion, your father likes to be dapper, a smart fellow, nicely turned out. He adopts a Frankie Vaughan sort of style, with Frankie Vaughan sort of hair. But his hands give him away. Industrial hands. They hurt when he hits you.

Do what your mother tells you, he says.

If your mother has just celebrated her twenty-third birthday, then you must be four years and seven months old, your father forty-six. It is July 1964, and he must now work extra hours to pay for the radiogram, whether or not she will have any use for it. Overtime is always available. It seems there will always be work in the Works.

On twelve hour nights he is required to clock-on at ten in the evening and finish at ten the next morning, after which he will sleep until tea-time. The day shift begins at six in the morning and ends at six in the evening, giving him the rest of the evening to sit in front of the television. But a twelve-hour back shift runs from two in the afternoon until two in the morning and means he must return home on the night bus, which tours most of the town and does not deliver him to the end of your street until some time after three – so late, or so early, that you are permitted to sleep all that week with your mother, allowing him to change out of his work-clothes without disturbing you, and climb into your bed without waking her.

At seven-thirty each evening Mummy settles you into her bed, in the room where you were born. She draws the curtains on the brightness outside and wishes you goodnight and leaves the door a few inches open. You listen to her slippers descending the stairs. Smiling, you roll onto your side and close your eyes, and at seven or so the next morning you wake to find her sleeping beside you.

Snug in the yeasty, warm fug of her, and conscious of the size of her comforting bottom, you conceive on one of these mornings the idea that you might place your hand where your father placed his.

Mummy is facing away from you. Her nightdress is white, dully luminous in the tented half-light of the sheets, a sheer nylon 'shortie' that has ridden up over her panties, which are Bri-Nylon and blue. You match your hand to the curve of one buttock, and she does not rebuke you; she does not move or make any noise, and you must suppose that she is asleep, entirely unconscious of what you are doing. For a minute or more you explore with your fingertips the shape of her bottom, its softness and scale. Babies come from ladies' bottoms. You shuffle closer and touch your peter against her. If it is possible for a child of your age to gain an erection, then you must be erect. If it is possible for you to know how babies are made, then you are making a baby. The tip of your tiny penis is touching Mummy's bottom through her Bri-Nylon panties, and still she does not stir.

You listen to her breathing; you listen to the milk-float in your street. The bottles rattle in their crates. They clink as the milkman sets them down. The motor whirrs as the float pulls away.

Eventually, satisfied, now fully awake, you slip from Mummy's bed and take yourself through to the toilet. You wee for a long time, and remember to pull the flush when you have finished. Then you go from there to your own bedroom so that you may look in on this man who may or may not be your father: his hairy shoulders and arms, the incongruous bulk of him under your bedclothes.

He might be a dead man, dumped in your bed. Despite the rush of water in the pipes, he is oblivious. You step closer. Your bedroom is rank with the smell of the Works, and when you prod him he does not open his eyes. He does not appear to be breathing. In your imagination you will have killed him. This thought may never leave you.

Peter! Come out of there! whispers Mummy, now wearing her dressing gown and holding your sister. Gladly you comply. Quietly she closes the door. She shuts your father into your bedroom, and allows you to lead her downstairs to the living room. Swinging your arms like a soldier, you take her through to the kitchen, where you sit on your stool at the yellow-topped table and wait with hands clasped to be given your Weetabix, your Quaker Oats or Rice Krispies, your Frosted Flakes or Sugar Pops.

At this age, your life is lived in the present. You do not think 'what next?' but 'what now?' You haven't yet acquired any sense of the shape or length of a life, and cannot look back on yourself from some imagined place in the future, when these days in your life will have passed. You cannot think of your present as a story yet to be told.

Your games, like your drawings and daydreams, are spun from a mind that does not yet know or expect to remember itself. Every day, without realising it, you are displacing the boy you were yesterday; every day you are forgetting him.

And just as you haven't yet memorised the days of the week – and have no conception of months – so you have yet to learn how to tell the time from the clock on the wall in your kitchen. A Smith's 'Dubarry' electric, the minute and hour hands progress imperceptibly, the second hand never stops circling, and the time is whatever Mummy or Daddy tell you it is.

It is time for your bath now, or time you calmed down. It is dinner-time; tea-time. Ten o'clock. Four o'clock. It is time to get ready for school.

When am I going to school?

Tomorrow, I told you, says Mummy.

She kneels by the side of the bath and presses the white rubber plug into the plughole. As a special treat, to mark the occasion of your becoming a schoolboy, she twists open a bottle of bubble bath and tips a blob of green gloop onto the point where the twin streams from the taps hit the enamel. You and your sister stand naked and watch as she swirls the water to generate a froth that soon covers most of the surface. Your sister squeals, excited, and Mummy dabs some bubbles on the tip of her nose.

And me, you say.

And you, she says, and deposits a scoop of white froth on top of your head. You laugh; your sister laughs too. Then Mummy pulls up one sleeve of her jersey and leans over the side of the tub. She tests the temperature by dipping her elbow through a gap in the bubbles. You are no longer too small to climb into or out of the bath, but you want Mummy to lift you over the rim. She lifts your sister in, too. You go first; your sister goes second. There can be no variation on this.

Is Lorraine going to school?

Your sister's name, then, is Lorraine. Let's settle on that.

No, says Mummy, she is too young for school. Only big boys and big girls go to school.

Does Keith from next door go to school?

Yes. Keith goes to school.

Will he play with me?

I am sure he will play with you.

Reassured by this, you sit in your wet cloud of bubbles while Mummy rests at the side of the tub. She lays one arm on the rim and pillows her face on her arm and sadly she watches as the bubbles melt slowly away, leaving islands of froth that you gather in close to your belly, until they too diminish and vanish.

Mummy sighs.

It is time now for her to wash your hair. She folds a flannel so that each of you in turn can press it to your eyes as she scoops and pours cup after cup of warm water onto your head to rinse off the suds. Your eyes are squeezed tight, since the shampoo will sting, and if either of you should feel the nip of it you will scream, and continue to scream until Mummy has doused the flannel in cold water and pressed it to the site of the calamity.

There, she says at last, lifting you out. Nice and clean for school.

But not Lorraine.

No, not Lorraine, she agrees, and wraps you in a towel and pats you dry, then hugs the soft warm bundle of your body, aged four and three quarters, which will soon be lost to you, and to her, as surely as the boy who inhabits it.

This must be why she is crying.

Your sister, meanwhile, unobserved, still sitting in the bath, has released a poo into the water. The jobby bobs up to the surface, and she starts to wail, another calamity.

Your town is polynucleated. In each of the housing estates there is a neighbourhood centre, a precinct of shops, a couple of churches, a cluster of schools. The schools benefit from spacious locations, broad horizons; this far from the Works, they benefit from clean air.

For instance, Bawdeswell Infants: a single-storey, flat-roofed construction of prefabricated grey and green panels, white-painted clapboard and glass. The two-storey Junior School is situated beside it, but has a separate entrance, its own black-barred metal gate, while a third, much larger gate opens onto a walkway that leads up to the campus of Bawdeswell Comprehensive: the Seniors.

If you are to become older – truly a big boy – you will need to progress from the first to the second to the third gate. In this way, your life has been planned for you.

The buildings are surrounded by fields, acres of flatness that stretch as far as the main arterial road on the western edge of the town. Twin white water towers mark the horizon. Cars go by, tractors and lorries, long intervals between them. There is farmland in the distance, open countryside, woodland, a landscape you have yet to encounter, that lies further into your boyhood, your future. For now, you must enter the Infants, following your mother and your sister in her new pushchair, across an asphalt playground in which stands a white flagpole. You look up at the flag, a Union Jack. Briefly it stirs. The sky scuds with cloud.

The date is Monday 21 September 1964. This is the day on which the island of Malta will gain its independence – not that you know this, not that your mother much cares. History happens elsewhere; it is happening always. More important to you and your mother is that today is the day on which you are to start school. This auspicious event, once contained in your future, has sped forward to meet you, and as you enter the building a kindly smiling lady, her hands on her knees, leans forwards to greet you. Her skirt is brown tweed, her cardigan green.

This must be Peter, she says, and asks if you like trains. You smile; shyly you nod. It seems you are to be given the gift of a train-set to welcome you into school life, and eagerly you follow her down a low-ceilinged corridor to an area of coat-pegs, each one marked by a picture on a rectangle of card. Until you learn how to read, the teacher explains, your peg will be the one displaying this picture of a train, a blue and red steam engine. Will you remember that, Peter?

The disappointment sets you to crying, and you continue to cry as you are led towards your first classroom, which is already busy with children. No one looks at you. Your mother has gone.

Again she has left you, but she will come back in a little while. She always comes back in a little while. You are given some paper and crayons and invited to sit at a table.

In this way your education begins with a let-down, abandonment, tears – a small lesson in life – but nevertheless you will discover, within a matter of days, that you are well-suited to school, its patterns, routines, the praise you receive, and each afternoon at three-forty, the bell ringing for home-time, you will spill with your classmates into the playground, eagerly seeking your mother's face among the melee of other mothers and pushchairs and prams at the gate. You will have so much to tell her. And she will be there, staring straight back at you, her face as inevitable as your reflection. She will speak to no one until finally you come out to rejoin her, and then, as your school-friends disperse, quickly forgotten, you will begin to describe your day in the school, and she will hear you, every word, and will not speak, because your mother exists only to hear what you have to tell her.

1965

Upwards you grow

S OON YOU WILL forget to say goodbye in the mornings in your hurry to find your friends and get on with the day. And soon your mother will stop walking you up to the school, or waiting at the gates to collect you.

Aged five, in 1965, you are already a big boy. You can walk yourself to school and back on your own. There are children everywhere, on every pavement, walking to and from the Infants, Juniors and Seniors. Four times every day, dinner time included, the pavements are as busy as the streets in and out of the Works. For the rest of the day they are empty.

The journey takes you twenty minutes and there are several possible routes, numerous combinations of streets and side-streets and shortcuts, and while much of this, the newest part of the new town, is designed to separate pedestrian from vehicular traffic, you must nevertheless cross two roads at least, or as many as five, depending on the line you find yourself following, the drift of your thoughts. Often you daydream.

The roads are not busy. Cars at this time are few. But you must be careful and remember the code. At school you have been inducted into the Tufty Club, and have learned to recite Tufty's road-crossing instructions. You wear a tin badge showing Tufty the fluffy-tailed squirrel, and quietly you chant to yourself at each kerbside, *Look right, look left, look right again, and if nothing is coming, no need to start running, walk straight across. . . .*

You do it correctly, and you are annoyed with the children who don't follow Tufty's code and yet avoid being knocked down and run over. In your imagination the cars and buses and lorries do not merely collide with pedestrians, but roll smoothly over them, flattening them into the tarmac. You hope this happens to the children who do not look left and right as they ought to. It will teach them a lesson.

Miss Whittle, it will teach them a lesson, Miss, won't it?

All of your teachers are female, and in time you will not remember any of them, neither their names nor their faces, with the exception of the headmistress, Miss Whittle, who is white-haired and sharp-featured, with a thin rasping voice that might, were she to shout, become a screech. But she does not shout; she does not need to, since every child in the school is afraid of her. If she were to appear in a story, such as your teacher reads aloud to your class on a Friday, she would be the witch, the stepmother, the wicked one.

Every morning in assembly the children sit cross-legged on the parquet floor of the hall to say their prayers and sing hymns, then distractedly listen to Miss Whittle's lectures, such as the story of the mother she observed just the previous day, who wanted to cross the road outside St Christopher's, the Catholic church.

This mother had come from the school next to the church, a Catholic mother with too many children to care for. There were two children holding the hem of her coat, and another two children sitting up in a pram, and she pushed the pram out ahead of her, straight into the traffic, which was so thoughtless and dangerous of her, wasn't it, children?

The Catholic mother ought to have found a zebra crossing, and if there wasn't a zebra crossing to be found she ought to have looked left, looked right, looked left again, then crossed the road ahead of the pram, pulling it after her. Some of the children who sit listening this morning will have little brothers and sisters of their own, and these children are to remind their mothers how to cross the road safely, unlike the example of the poor Catholic mother.

Will you do that, children?

Yes, Miss!

But you won't. You will keep from your own Catholic mother this important information that may save your sister from being knocked down and run over, crushed flat in her pushchair.

On Thursdays you have your weekly session of Music, Movement and Mime. The school caretaker carries a reel-to-reel tape deck into your classroom while you are at assembly. He is still there when you file back in through the door. Grunting, red-faced, he moves the desks and chairs to the edge of the room. Your teacher waits for him to leave, then shuts the door behind him and pulls down the blind.

Good! she says, and inserts the plug in the socket and instructs you and the other children to strip to your pants and vests and pull on your plimsoles. She stands to one side of the tape deck and operates the controls while facing the class. There is music, and a woman's voice speaking over the music, and your teacher calling out words of encouragement.

You must pretend to be a tree in a forest. You begin life as a tiny acorn, crouched low. Then comes the sunshine, followed by rain. Upwards you grow. You stretch and reach for the sky. Your fingers are leaves, rustling in the breeze; your arms are branches, swaying in the wind.

Well done, Natalie, calls your teacher, that is very good!

Disheartened, your arms sinking, you look over your shoulder at Natalie, who is so much better at being a tree than you are. She is on tiptoes. Her cotton vest is white, like yours; her knickers are navy. She wears knee-length white socks and black elasticated plimsoles. Her hair is dark and short, her mouth plump and small. Her second name is Hayes.

Concentrate now! says your teacher, clapping her hands. Peter, look to the front, please.

You are conscientious, a good boy. Excellent work is to be re-warded with a gold or silver star and the privilege of sticking the star to the chart on the wall, which displays the progress of each child in the class. Already Natalie Hayes has more gold and silver stars than anyone else. Red stars are to be given for effort, blue for best behaviour, and already you have the most red and blue stars.

At this age you have a predilection for modelling in plasticine, and today you are making a budgerigar in a cage, but the cage starts to sag before you can complete it, the browned plasticine softened with handling. Natalie stands by your elbow.

It's good, she says; I like your budgie a lot.

Me too, you say.

Maurice, what are you drawing? she asks in a teacherly voice.

Across the table sits a pale, scruffy boy in a green knitted jersey. He is scribbling in crayons, furiously colouring in. A house, he replies. But each of its windows is circular. You point out to him that the windows in houses are square, and Maurice smiles as if from far away, then attacks his sheet of paper with renewed vigour, creating another swirl, another window.

Miss, you complain, raising your arm.

But your teacher is kinder to Maurice than he surely deserves, and confirms that windows in houses may sometimes be round, just as they are on boats, when they are called portholes. Unhappily, uncertainly, you accept the idea of round windows in houses, because she is a grown-up, and your teacher.

I've seen round windows, says Natalie; I've seen them on holiday.

Have you? smiles your teacher.

You are each to bring to school a small box or a tin. In her encouraging voice your teacher says, Put up your hand if your grandad smokes a pipe or rolls his own cigarettes.

These children, she says, are the lucky ones. If they ask their grandads nicely they may be allowed to have one of his empty tobacco tins. And if they ask him especially nicely they may be allowed to have two tins, one for themselves and one for their teacher, who can share the extra tins with the unlucky children whose grandads do not smoke a pipe or roll their own cigarettes.

Will you do that for me? she says. Will you ask your grandads nicely?

Yes, Miss, reply the lucky ones.

They are smiling, but you are not one of the lucky ones, and neither is Maurice. You watch their arms come down, then leave your chair to share with your teacher the fact that one of your grandads is dead – he died before you were born, the one who lived up in Glasgow – while the other one lives far away, on the island of Malta. You are not sure if you have met him, but as you explain your situation you decide that he must be a pipe smoker, a kindly old man who would surely donate his empty tobacco tins if only he knew they were needed.

Go back to your chair now, Peter, she says.

The tin is to keep your words in.

One afternoon, a week or so later, your teacher calls you to her desk and presents you with a tin that smells faintly of raisins, perhaps also of rust, the screws or nails it may once have contained. Inside you discover a selection of single-syllable starter words – *cat, hat, tree, see* – which she has written out on coloured card in evenly-spaced letters identical to those displayed on the charts pinned around the walls of the classroom: *Aa is for apple,*

Bb is for bee. She has snipped the card, a single word to each small coloured rectangle, and she has done this for each of the thirty-eight children she teaches.

In the months to come you will learn to write your own words, and to cut out your own bits of card – two syllables, three syllables – and to join them up into sentences, then into stories, but for now you are mesmerized by this gift, each word as special as if it were a sixpence.

Eager to share the tin with your mother, you hurry down the hill from the Infants at home-time, sunlight shimmering in the chain-link fence to your right, the wind loud in your ears, and continue on past the house where Natalie Hayes lives, then up as far as the turn for Bawdeswell Avenue, which is where you step straight into the road, not thinking to pause to look left and right, your mind being so absorbed in practising your words, which scatter in the shock of the car that just misses you, its noise and suddenness, the rush of exhaust as it goes.

You did not see it coming; you did not predict it.

Your tin and its lid clatter on the tarmac. Your bits of card skitter away in the breeze, and helplessly you watch as two older boys chase after them, jostling each other in their duffel coats.

One of the boys is Keith from next door. He and his friend are laughing, and they ought to be careful. They should not be messing about in the road. Cars can be deadly. But no more cars are coming, and your bewilderment is not just surprise that something so unexpected has happened, but that you have not been knocked down and run over.

The car was bottle-green, a family saloon, and as it passes from view it takes with it a story in which you are flattened to the road and your future self does not come to exist, in which your end arrives early. You ought to have been given a lesson. Your older self will think of this often and wonder perhaps if you were.

Keith Coatley returns the pieces of card to your tin, his friend gives you the lid, and because you are crying they stand and observe you, but no words are spoken. You wait until they decide to move on, still jostling, then you cross over the road, remembering now to look left and right, and when you reach the far pavement you break into a run, and run all the way home, overtaking Keith and his friend, who are dawdling.

Safe in your mother's bright yellow kitchen you don't mention what has just happened, but thrust the tin at her as she stands at the sink, her hands submerged in a blue plastic bucket. Your sister abandons her toys and comes to see what you have brought home from the school. Mummy wrings a grey cloth and finally looks down at you, frowning.

What is the matter? she says.

It seems you are still crying, and you dare not say anything. She glances to your tin, which you don't want to share with your sister, who is reaching to take it. These are your words, not hers.

What is the matter, Peter, she says with impatience; tell me, what is this, what are you showing me?

But you cannot explain it. Instead you turn to your sister and push her away; you push her so hard you make her fall over.

Peter! shouts Mummy, and you feel the wet from her hand on your cheek, a sudden smell of drains and detergent.

There are no books in your house, and no stories at bedtime, except for the tales you tell to yourself, which continue into your sleep, becoming your dreams, becoming something like memories: for instance the night your grandmother comes into your bedroom, such a short, dumpy old soul, a fat book in her hand. She wants to read you a story, and sits heavily on the edge of the mattress, trapping you snugly inside the blankets. In a slow, mumbling voice, hunched over the book, lamplight glinting in her spectacles, she reads to you from the Holy Bible, not a word of it familiar, none of it English, and when she is finished she closes the book with something like reverence, something like affection, stroking its cover. Then sighing, she kisses your forehead and says God bless, a phrase that no one else in your family will ever use, since no one goes to church or says their prayers; besides which, they so rarely use terms of endearment.

You will not be able to place this memory, or conjure any other details of her visit, and will be obliged to distrust it, a story you have invented, since both your parents will deny it can ever have happened.

I don't think so, your mother will say in her accent; my mother is passed away, and your other grandma has not been here.

No, she's never been down here, your father will add, with certainty; not in my house, not in this fucking house.

There are no books, and no talk of religion, but it is some time around now, in 1965, that your mother decides that you should go to the Sunday School in the hall next to St Christopher's. She has spoken to Mrs McIllaney from number 41, whose daughters Bernie and Mary are waiting outside on the pavement, dressed in their Sunday best clothes: identical blue pinafores and grey knitted cardigans, clean white socks, tan buckle shoes. Bernadette is older, a big girl; Mary is your age, though taller, and wears an embroidered white headband in the dark pudding-bowl of her hair.

The girls are holding hands. Just half an hour ago you were alone on the lawn at the front of your house, blowing seeds from a dandelion, when your mother said it was time to come inside and get ready – for what, she did not say – and now you too are dressed in your Sunday best clothes, your white socks and brown leather sandals, blue cotton shorts, blue cable-knit jumper.

The girls wait, but you are seized with a determination not to go with them, not to go near to the Catholic church. You cling to the cold metal pole that supports the porch at the front of your house. Screaming, you refuse to let go of the pole and when your mother summons your father – this man who must be your father – you know it is already too late for you: there is no letting go, and you have no choice now but to be punished.

And possibly that is what imprints this event in your memory. It is not merely the fear of your father and the certainty that you will be spanked, but your sudden awareness of yourself as a boy who is screaming. Here is your mother, retreating into the hallway as if to escape you, and here is your sister, standing beside her. Here are the McIllaney girls, holding hands in the sunshine, and here is Peter, aged five and two thirds, clutching tight to this pole and creating such a commotion.

There is this, and the eventual surprise of your father's good humour. A newspaper is folded under his arm, *The People*. As he comes through from the living room he looks at you and laughs. I don't think he wants to go, he says, and grins at your mother. Doesn't look like he's interested, he adds, then steps around her and climbs the stairs to the toilet. He laughs again, and your mother slams the front door on you, as if to be done with you.

Days later you wake to the sound of a tussle at the foot of the stairs. You were fast asleep, and now your eyes are wide open. You are staring at the pattern in the curtains that you will trace with your eyes every morning and evening across all the years of your childhood, and will never remember. You follow the shapes in the fabric and listen to your parents downstairs in the hallway, where your father is wrestling to keep hold of your mother, who is whimpering, drunk. She says she wants to go to bed now; she wants to be left on her own. She sounds like a little girl. Your father sounds like her father. Perhaps he will spank her.

Come on, behave yourself, he says. Dolly, come on.

Let me go! she complains. Let me go!

Dolly, we have guests, he growls. You can't just fuck off to bed.

She is making a show of herself; she is showing him up. She will not do what he tells her to. But when she starts to wail he has to release her. Sobbing, she clambers upstairs and bursts into their bedroom, slamming this door after her too. She falls onto the bed, and her cries become muffled. Downstairs your father makes his apologies, and you hear a man, then a woman, both of them strangers. They had best be heading off, they say. And he isn't to worry, not at all. It has been a great night.

The front door clicks shut behind them. There is silence. Time passes. Then your father returns to the living room and you let yourself sink back into sleep.

Later their voices are vicious. They are just the other side of your wall. This may be a different night, for your mother is no longer whimpering, and your father no longer sounds like her father. Take your hands away from me, she says; I am warning you. There is a blow, and your father exclaims: You bugger! He is winded, in pain. You suppose she has struck him again in the joe, as she did once before, when they were shouting downstairs in the kitchen.

That was a tea-time, and you watched as he backed into the living room, clutching his privates. Mummy was dressed to go out, and brandishing a stool, its four metal legs bristling.

Of course your father didn't retaliate, but allowed your mother to leave. She is fiery, like Shirley Bassey, and he is a gentleman; everyone says so. No matter how much she might provoke him, he will not lift a hand to her. Many times, returning from work, he will clip you round the ear, or give you a clout on the backside, if Mummy should complain about your behaviour. And many times, too, he will cuff the back of your head if you are cheeky, or clumsy, or bothering your sister. But you will not see him spanking Lorraine, or hitting your mother. Your father was a soldier, a sergeant, and does not hit women or girls.

Instead he will shout, and your mother will shout back at him.

They are shouting now, and you cannot bear it, or make any sense of it. You lie under your covers, your pillows over your ears, but still you can hear them. Angrily you hurl back your bedclothes and hammer on the wall with your fists. Be quiet! you plead; Mummy, Daddy, stop shouting!

Go to sleep, yells Mummy; mind your own business!

But that is an end to it. For a little while longer they continue shouting in whispers, then trail off into silence, exhausted. You lie very still. If you move, or make any sound, you might rouse them once more. You close your eyes. Minutes later you hear the creak of their mattress. It creaks again. The creaking develops a rhythm, like breathing; it lulls you to sleep.

Of course, other grown-up things happen at night, and in the morning you and your sister will find them cuddling in the kitchen, your father chuckling, your mother smiling as though to herself. She will be wearing her white 'shortie' nightdress, her legs bared to the top of her thighs, her red knickers exposed. The nightdress is nylon, double-layered, 20 denier over 30 denier, and appears to be transparent, though you cannot see through it, and neither can your father. He is looking. She turns away from him. He continues to stare, and you and Lorraine sit on your stools and wait for your breakfast, after which everything is just as it ought to be, exactly as it usually is, at least for a little while.

Another day; it is evening. The front door slams. Your mother walks across from your pavement to the opposite pavement. She does not look left or right, but hurries towards the end of your long curving street in her high heels, slim calves, her short angry strides. The skirt she wears is brand new, tight and zipped at the side; the herringbone jacket is matching. Both are lined in red rayon satin. These are her catalogue clothes, the ones you helped her to choose.

Peter, this one, or that one?

That one.

Yes, I think so. F, not E. She folded the edge of the page. You must not tell your father.

No, you said; it's a secret.

A secret, she confirmed, and pretended to zip tight your mouth.

But now you must watch as she stalks from the house in her new clothes, the outfit you helped her to choose. Your chin is level with the window ledge, which smells of Pledge and the rot that has begun to eat into the timber: condensation. Your sister stands beside you, and looks up at your father, who is lighting a cigarette. Where is Mummy going? she asks him.

To see her fancy man, he says.

Her fancy man. You imagine a black man. You haven't yet seen a black man, not in your new town, only on television, but this is a phrase you know you have heard: oh, she's run away with the black man.

When is she coming back?

Your father does not say. Perhaps he hasn't the sense to reassure you; perhaps he intends that you and your sister should feel the pain of this moment as he is feeling it, and forever blame her, your mother, for abandoning her husband and children. Your older self will suppose so, though as your mother hurries away from your house you fear the blame must also be yours, for helping her choose her new outfit, for keeping her secrets, since of course you are too young to see that the fault must be your father's, for refusing ever to leave your neat house to go dancing, or to the pub, or even to walk once a while in the sunshine.

Come on, he says then, up to bed now; and though it is still light outside, and surely too early for bedtime, both you and your sister comply. You do as he tells you to, this man whose young wife has just left him.

Daddy, you ask; do you know Chicken Licken?

What's that?

We learned it at school, you say. It's a story. It makes me frightened.

Just go to sleep now, he tells you.

In the morning she is still gone. You sense this as soon as you wake and hear your father coughing downstairs, the kettle beginning to whistle. Possibly he has sat up all night in the kitchen, smoking cigarettes and drinking cups of tea, perhaps whisky or beer, polishing his shoes, putting labels on things, waiting for your mother to come back to him.

Their bed has not been slept in. The pillows are neatly aligned, two perfect white mounds. The curtains are open. Sunlight gleams on the bedspread, which is rayon satin too, peachy and metallic. It glints in her scent bottles, which are gathered on the dressing table, huddled like people, like toys.

Peter, they are not toys. They are not for playing with. Leave them alone now.

Quietly you enter the room. The smell of her lingers, warmed by the sunshine. Everything is tidy, carpeted, clean. On many other mornings you have wandered in here to watch as Mummy dresses herself in her undergarments: her white conical bra and elastic s-t-r-e-t-c-h panties, suspenders, tan stockings, white nylon slip. Sometimes she will lift you onto the bed and turn her back and ask you to pull up her zip. Sometimes you and your sister will sit together on the edge of the bed, legs dangling, and watch as she applies her make-up, her reflection tripled in the dressing-table mirrors. The transformation will be subtle. Even when she applies her red lipstick, making such shapes with her mouth, her face will still be Mummy's.

What do you think? she will ask you. How do I look?

Nice, you will say, because Mummy will always look nice, with or without her make-up.

Your sister will slide down then from the mattress, and stand with her arms at her sides, her face tilted upwards. This will be her treat, because she is a girl: a dab of foundation on her cheeks and forehead, a smear of red lipstick. The change in her will be startling, and you will resent it.

But now Mummy is gone, and Daddy is downstairs in the kitchen, smoking and drinking his tea, perhaps something stronger, since your father likes to take a wee nip. This is another phrase you have heard.

The noise he makes sounds like Mummy when she is crying, though your father cannot be crying. Dads do not cry. You go to sit on her stool, expecting to be joined by a crowd of yourself, captured in her cluster of mirrors. But the outer panes are not angled far enough inwards. You hinge the side-mirrors towards you and your many reflections lean with you, some of them the other way. You see the back of your head, the swirl of hair round your crown, the slender line of your neck. You confront yourself in the middle mirror, nose to nose. Your face is smooth and unblemished, your eyes large and clear. You are a boy. The face in the mirror copies your face exactly. Whatever expression you pull, you cannot surprise it.

Your mother keeps her cosmetics in the smallest of the drawers, beneath the main mirror. You rummage among her lipsticks for the one that is the most red. The cylindrical lid slides smoothly off. The notched dial in the base causes the stick to spiral out. Experimentally you apply some colour to your mouth, then look for her bottle of mascara. The brush is integral to the cap, the bristles claggy with black, which you paint onto your eyebrows. Her silvery compact has a sprung catch that clicks when you open it. Inside it conceals another mirror, and a circular pad dusty with powder. You dab your cheeks, then smear your forehead and chin.

The boy in the mirrors has ceased to resemble you, but still smiles when you do, pouts when you pout.

There are drawers on either side of the dressing table. In the bottom left you will find her catalogues, in the bottom right a hairdryer wrapped in its cable, a scatter of grips, a polythene bag of spiked plastic rollers in pink, yellow and blue. A narrow drawer contains her jewellery box, with its tangle of bracelets and beads. The other drawers contain her underwear. One is cushiony with stockings and tights, biscuit-coloured, and smelling of biscuits, faintly of perfume. Her bras and belts occupy another drawer, soft cups inside cups. You know what you are looking for, her red nylon panties. They are cool and slinky, liquid in your hands. You pull them up over your pyjama bottoms. The matching bra is flimsier than the other bras. You hook your arms through the straps, then stand on her stool to examine your reflection. Your pyjamas are cotton, patterned with a motif of racing cars. Even wearing her make-up and underwear, you do not resemble your mother, who has abandoned you.

Peter, get down from there, says your father.

He is standing in the doorway, a cigarette in his mouth. She has abandoned him, too. Poor Daddy. He stands sideways on and reaches one arm towards you, as if afraid he might glimpse himself in the mirrors, his paunch and grey stubble, the sad slope of his eyes. Come on, he says softly; let's get you ready for school.

You are a big boy, and brave, unafraid of high places. You leap from the stool to the carpet and run to your father, who is not cross with you, not always.

1966

children fall often

HERE YOU ARE in your living room, half-kneeling on a grey acrylic carpet that will soon need replacing: it is becoming threadbare, and is rucked near the skirting board. It came with the house, a Corporation floor-covering with the thinnest of underlay. Mummy will not put up with it for much longer. If Daddy wants her to stay here, he will need to pay for a new one.

The year is 1966: this will be your best guess. The camera angle is low, cropping the cards on the sideboard, which may well be your birthday cards at the start of that year, or some Christmas cards at the end of it. Either you are just six, or else nearly seven. Your future self, looking back at yourself, will not be able to tell. But you will remember the gift of this petrol station: a scale-model garage in painted hardboard, complete with pump stands, forecourt sign, and vehicle ramp. Whether or not it was delivered by

Santa, you know it was made by Ken Coatley, who has carried it through from next door. Ken makes them in the shed in his garden; you have heard him tapping and sawing.

Ken is good with his hands, everybody says so.

Keith Coatley is kneeling beside you. There is a Matchbox replica car in your right hand, and a line of other vehicles queuing to come in to the garage, including a Conqueror tank with a swivelling turret and a red Routemaster bus, a *Stingray* submarine, a covered wagon drawn by four horses.

The feet in the foreground must belong to Ken Coatley, who is sitting on the edge of the sofa, no doubt next to his wife, who is called Carole. You recognise their footwear: his brown suede Chelsea boots, her comfortable casuals.

Your mother is standing in the background, cropped at the waist, wearing her heels, and when in your future you return to re-examine this scene, not quite sure what more is to be found here, you will notice at last the blur of the budgerigar just behind her. It is clinging to the hem of the curtain, almost lost in the shadow cast by the camera flash.

Peter, look this way. Peter!

There has always been a budgerigar. At this time in England one in four homes has a budgerigar, and yours is named after your mother: Dolly Dolores. This was your choice, your father insists, though you have no memory of that. Dolly Dolores will have been there in her cage when you danced to the Yeah Yeahs, when Mummy and Daddy admired the radiogram, when you stood and watched Mummy hurrying away from the house, when at last she returned. Dolly Dolores has lived in your living room for longer than you are able to remember, and whatever you later recall of these years, you must not neglect to include the noise of the budgerigar.

Dolly's cage is tall and cylindrical, with a pale blue lid and base that correspond to her colouring. It stands on a black metal tripod in the corner of the room furthest from the television, nearest the draught from the back-garden window. Mummy worries about the draught, which is one reason she drapes the budgie beneath a bedsheet at night. The other is to silence her.

Peter, you are tormenting that bird!

I'm not, I'm teaching her to talk.

Aged six, perhaps seven, you will sometimes elevate yourself to Dolly Dolores's height by using the leatherette pouffe that Mummy has bought from the furniture floor of the Co-operative Department Store in the town centre. The pouffe will wheeze when you stand on it. Mummy will warn you to be careful. Yes, you will say, then keep very still, as still as a statue, just like your teacher has taught you in school, in Music, Movement and Mime.

Dolly Dolores is rarely still, seldom quiet. The wires that enclose her shimmer with her constant activity. Under your gaze she will hop along the middle of her three perches, her scaly claws gripping the balsa wood, to batter her mirror with her hooked little beak, seemingly affronted by the appearance of another budgerigar, exactly like her. Angrily, too, she will scatter the seeds in her tray, or peck at her cuttlefish, or rattle her bell. Then as she hangs from her long thread of millet you might ease your finger through the wires and attempt to stroke her soft crown.

You are patient, a diligent boy, and you take seriously the task of coaxing Dolly Dolores to talk. Your father has shown you how it ought to be done. First you must wait until you have gained her trust and attention; then you must repeat the same sounds over and over. There should be no variation, you must not confuse her:

Dolly Dolores, Dolly Dolores, Dolly Dolores. . . .

You believe it will help if you adopt the strangulated voice of a budgerigar. And when from time to time she appears to respond you will claim that these trills and squawks are an echo of the words that you have just taught her.

You are her teacher; she must do as you tell her. Seen through Dolly Dolores's eyes you will resemble a grown-up. But you are also her friend. Released from her cage, Dolly Dolores will swoop from curtain to curtain, then onto the backs of the chairs, and finally from there to your shoulder, yours in preference to anyone else's.

There are no photographs to prove this.

You will communicate with Dolly in budgerigar noises as you coax her onto the perch of your finger. Mummy and Lorraine will be watching you. That's the way, your father will say.

Slowly, carefully, you will bring Dolly round to face you, and if she does not take fright, or hop into your hair, she may permit you to kiss her. Then slowly, carefully, you will lower her towards your other hand, which will be waiting. You must not startle her, you must not be clumsy. Your hand will enclose her, and her heart will be fluttering. The black beads of her eyes will be terrified.

If you were to squeeze very hard you might crush her. All the bones in her body would be broken. You would have killed her. It would be so easy.

Peter, shall we put Dolly back in her cage now?

Yes, please, you will say.

Dolly Dolores appears in one other photograph, confined to her cage, a pale blue smear in the background. If the photo commemorates an occasion, the picture gives no clue as to what that might be. You are captured with Mummy, whose hand is resting on your shoulder. She is not smiling. Neither are you.

Bars of sunlight show through the slats in the blinds, and the curtains are open. It is daytime. It may well be the summer, the last before your sister starts school. Let us settle on that: the summer of 1966, when England will win the World Cup, though this is not an event that you will be aware of, not yet. So many things will occur that you are not aware of.

Lorraine is nearly four and a half, and stands slightly off to one side, as though she has just wandered into the frame. Perhaps your father has called to her. She is turning her head, preparing to smile for him – for his Kodak Brownie 44 – though unwittingly, too, she is presenting herself to your gaze, offering herself to the scrutiny of an adult who does not yet exist but will one day return to this image, half-hoping to find that some small thing may have changed.

The details are distracting. Both you and your sister are dressed in white ankle socks, T-bar sandals and shorts. Her collared tee-shirt has stripes; you have the chubbier knees. Your mother's Courtelle cardigan is buttoned to the neck and her slacks are hemmed an inch or two above the ankle. She wears open-toed mules with dark socks, and her hair is styled shorter, showing her ears. Her spectacles resemble swimming goggles, a pair of thick-rimmed ovals.

What else? On the dark-veneered sideboard is displayed a young rubber plant with half a dozen leaves, and a ruby-red vase in the shape of an oversized brandy glass, and a pair of teak antelopes, one taller than the other. The living room wallpaper has a pattern of stylised bulrushes and leaves, and the curtains have a similar theme, some kind of foliage.

Nothing here but the budgerigar will remain in your memory, or survive your mother's restlessness; everything you can see in this picture will be replaced.

Always on her excursions around the living room Dolly Dolores will deposit little plips, tiny nuggets of black and creamy white that your mother will collect on the tip of a butter knife that she keeps for this purpose. She will smear the knife in a Kleenex, her face pinched, holding her breath, despite the fact that Dolly's plips have no smell – you have put your nose to one – unlike her cage, which will stink if left for too long, the sheets of *Pink'Un* lining its base made claggy with droppings. It is Mummy who cleans out the cage, and Mummy who decides when Dolly should be allowed to fly free.

Mummy, can Dolly Dolores come out now?

She is not listening. You tug at her sleeve.

Mummy?

Peter, go and play. Why are you not playing with Andrew?

But you have already been playing with Andrew, who is lying on his belly on the carpet, running a motor car in and out of the garage that Ken Coatley has made for your birthday, possibly Christmas. Your sister kneels a few feet away from him, not playing but watching, her hands in her lap.

They are in the corner by the birdcage, while here on this side of the room sits Andrew's mother, in the white wicker chair from your bedroom. Broad-bottomed, too wide in the hips to fit the confines of the seat, she sits slightly side-on, as if about to get to her feet. Her slacks are blue Terylene, stretched taut round her thighs, and her knees are parted for Deborah, her daughter, who lolls between them, sucking her thumb.

Deborah is one year younger than your sister, as Andrew is one year younger than you, and this is the first time they have been inside your house, though they live just two doors away. It is the first time, in fact, that you have seen so many women crowded into your living room: three on the settee, one in each of the armchairs, two on chairs carried through from the kitchen, your mother perched on the pouffe, Andrew's mother in the white wicker chair.

Her name is Sally Clough, and this gathering is called a Tupperware party. Among the other women you recognise Nadia, grown plumper, who cradles a baby, a bottle tilted into its mouth, and tiny, big-bosomed Annie Goldman, who has been to visit before, bringing her two daughters – Linda and Samantha – who are being looked after today by their grandma: you have asked, and she did not tease you for asking. She is your new favourite, nicer even than Nadia.

Carole Coatley from next door is not here; perhaps she is at work, serving in the bakers on the Lingwood Road precinct.

Perhaps she will come later; perhaps she and your mother have already had words.

Most of these women, including your mother, work part-time for the Corporation, as waitresses and cleaners in the Civic Centre Complex, though this is not yet something you know. All morning, it seems, they have they been talking and smoking and drinking their cups of coffee and tea, and your living room is now soupy with the smell of them, their dregs and cigarettes, perfume and hairspray. Whatever it is they are talking about, you are conscious only of the sound of it, how it swells and subsides, the sudden eruptions of laughter.

Urgently you whisper: Mummy?

But she leans away from you, handing something to Sally.

That's the children's supper tray, says the woman called Edna.

Sally nods, and dutifully tilts the tray to look at its underside.

Edna sucks on her cigarette. She is older than the others, and heavier, her face dusty with a powder that gives her complexion the same tint as her stockings. Sturdily she occupies the armchair by the television, an order book in her lap, and from where you are standing you can see up her skirt to her underwear. She looks at you, unsmiling; she closes her legs and tugs her skirt to her knees.

Not one of these women has yet seen your budgerigar fly across the room or settle on your shoulder. None of them has seen you return her to her cage.

Mummy, you try again, but she is not listening, and with a sigh of irritation you push away from her and step around the samples spread out on the carpet, the columns of multi-coloured beakers, stacks of side-plates and mixing bowls, the see-through lidded boxes whose special Tupperware seal locks in flavour and freshness, locks out moisture and dryness.

You have been warned not to touch them. You wouldn't want to anyway.

The latch on the cage door is easily sprung, though first you will need Ken Coatley's garage to stand on. Andrew helps you remove the cars from its roof, and your sister shuffles closer, as if she has been waiting for just this chance to join in. Together they stand to watch you. Lorraine's socks are grubby, you notice, dragging loose at the toes. She has taken off her best shoes, which your mother insisted she wear even though they're so stiff. They hurt her heels. She has to have plasters.

Conscious now of your own brand-new shoes, which have animal prints on the soles and a compass in one heel, you step onto the roof of the garage, which is not nearly as sturdy as you were expecting. Constructed with panel pins and glue, the walls shift slightly as you pull open the catch on the cage door. Holding your breath, you extend a finger towards Dolly Dolores, then suck in your cheeks to make a noise like a budgerigar. You wait. You make the noise again, and Dolly Dolores hops down. She nods and bobs. Carefully, importantly, you withdraw your hand, ease her out through the gap. But now you must shift your weight to turn round, and something cracks, the wood splinters; suddenly the walls of the garage tilt to one side and you find yourself falling.

But children fall often. Children are experts in falling, and when Dolly Dolores flies off you have no choice but to laugh, since Andrew is still watching you. Uh oh, you say, and make a silly face. Delighted, he smiles, and glances behind him.

Here comes Mummy; here comes another spanking.

Some of the women are squealing, some of them laughing, though not because of you: no one is looking your way. As Mummy yanks you upright you glimpse Dolly Dolores swooping over the women, passing through their scented air, inches from their hair-dos. Nadia cringes; Annie Goldman's laugh is like a scream. Sally Clough pulls Deborah towards her.

The first slap to your bottom makes you cry out, and as you try to pull away you notice some Tupperware plates spilling onto the carpet, their pretty pastel shades, where someone has kicked them. I didn't mean it! you plead, and twist to evade the next swipe of Mummy's hand, but the next swipe does not come. Exasperated, she releases your arm and hurries away from you, because Dolly Dolores has flown into the blinds. She is trapped between the slats, frantically flapping to get free, and the noise is frightening.

Oh! cries one of the women; its foot's all tangled up. Dolly, I don't know what to do.

'Dolly' means your mother, and no one, it seems, knows what to do, no one except you.

Dolly Dolores thrashes, then is calm. Suddenly she thrashes again. The women stand aside, and your mother decides not to touch her. Instead, she lets you come forward. With your supple, patient fingers you are able to loosen the cable in which the budgie's legs and claws are entangled, and though she cannot refrain from pecking at your hands, angry and alarmed as she must be, you bear this without flinching. It is after all your fault: you ought not to have opened her cage.

Consolingly you speak to Dolly Dolores in budgerigar noises.

Feathers float down, tiny blades of iridescent blue, scuts of fluffy white. She deposits a plip on your hand. One of her wings is oddly aligned, kinked where it shouldn't be. You notice this as you pass her contritely to Mummy. You dare not wipe the plip from your hand.

Annie Goldman squeezes your shoulder; then Edna announces that it is time to take down some orders, if the ladies are ready, since she must soon be leaving. She has not risen from her arm-chair, and as the ladies settle back in their seats she licks the end of her pen, squares the pad on her lap. Your mother steps around her. She carries Dolly Dolores across to her cage, and Nadia goes with her, still cradling her baby, who is called Ana.

Andrew and your sister are waiting by the wreckage of Ken Coatley's garage. You stand beside them, the tallest of the children, a big boy, though not yet big enough to see into the base of the birdcage, where Mummy sets down the budgerigar.

Poor little thing, says Nadia. She smiles at you sadly. It seems Dolly Dolores is unable to stand or fly up to her perch. I think she will have to be put to sleep, adds Nadia, her voice close to a whisper.

Your mother sucks in a breath. She nods, but doesn't seem certain.

Despite the commotion, Ana is now fast asleep in Nadia's arms, one fat cheek pillowed on her shoulder. Her moist lips continue to suckle. Nadia cups a hand to the back of her head and sways from side to side. You watch them. Then you say: I think Dolly should be put to sleep as well.

Your mother turns to look at you; she considers you closely.

As young as you are, you cannot have misunderstood them. Your older self, looking back at yourself, will doubt that you are innocent of what you have just said.

All right, your mother says then, and stoops to gather up the remains of the garage. Afterwards, in a little while, she says.

And once the last of these women has gone from your house, including Nadia, Mummy will gaze dismally around at the mess they have made in her living room, then step out of her heels and into her slippers, and collect all the cups and saucers and ashtrays from the carpet, and return all the chairs to their usual places, then lift the bird from its cage as if it were simply the next thing to be tidied. She will carry it through to the kitchen and place it on the metal tray she uses for cooking on Sundays. The budgie will skitter a little, but won't attempt to fly off, and your mother will not appear to notice you or your sister as she slides the tray into the oven and turns on the gas. The oven door will click as it closes. She won't press the ignition.

I am not hurting her, she will say. Dolly will go to sleep now, that is all. The gas will make her sleepy.

Is Mummy angry with you? The urgent hiss of the gas will make you think so, but when finally your sister complains about the smell, your mother will nod, as if she understands, and give a small smile, then continue to stare at the closed white door of the oven, apparently calm, which is when your father, arriving home from his shift, will come in by the back door and start shouting.

He will swear at her, and toss his cigarette outside, and hastily switch off the gas. He will fling open the windows and usher you and Lorraine into the living room, and shove your mother after you, then slam the door after her.

As if shaken awake, momentarily disorientated, your mother will absorb the fact of your two faces looking up at her, then open her arms and begin to whine, as if she were the little one, a little girl, younger even than Lorraine. Weakly she will embrace you, hopelessly you will embrace her, and that will be that, the end of Dolly Dolores.

A day or two later you will discover the budgie in the dustbin in the kitchen, wrapped in a single soiled sheet of the *Pink'Un*. Her head will be floppy, her eyes like tiny blisters, and while your future self will puzzle at your acceptance of this, aged six, perhaps seven years old, you will have no trouble adapting to your father's account of making such a botch of putting Dolly Dolores to sleep.

On several occasions over several years you will hear him tell this same story, another family favourite: how he laid Dolly Dolores on a baking tray inside the oven, the gas hissing but unlit, until the smell became so intense that he thought he might also suffocate, and opened the oven to retrieve the dead bird, a damp dish towel held over his nose, only for Dolly to make a sudden panicked attempt to escape, miraculously still able to fly. She arrowed straight for the garden but met the kitchen window instead, which resulted in her broken neck. She collided with the glass and dropped down dead. She landed on the window ledge.

You will listen to your father repeating this tale, and for a while you will even adopt it, grinning at the ironies. But though there are certain clear storylines you might one day follow out of that afternoon – your friendship with Andrew, for instance, and

the many other small creatures that will perish as a consequence
of it, or the holiday your family will take with the Goldmans, or
the memory of your mother carrying your demolished garage next
door to Ken Coatley, leaving you once again to look after Lorraine,
leaving you for a long time, or the sound of your father groaning
in the kitchen, a sound that only you are able hear, you feel sure,
or the noise of your mother, sobbing in her bedroom, once again
sobbing – for now you are just six, perhaps seven years old, and
clearly you cannot anticipate what may lie ahead of you, or begin
to make sense of what may already be happening.

1967

your father's favourite

YET HOW CLOSELY yours will come to resemble the ideal family of that time: father, mother, their two children (though not a dog; not yet a little dog). The father is some years older and some inches taller than his wife, who is so pretty. Their son is a few years older and a few inches taller than his sister. The boy dresses in shorts; the girl wears a short dress. The ribbon in the girl's hair matches the pattern in her mother's headscarf. The boy's hairstyle matches his father's, cut now to collar-length, still parted on the left.

Here you are in the adverts you see on the television, and here in the schoolbooks with which you are still learning to read: Janet and John.

This is Janet.

This is John.

Janet is the favoured one.

John must not put a foot wrong.

You strive to be admired because your sister is the favoured one. Your father prefers her, that much is clear, this man who may not be your father, this girl who looks so much like him. Everyone says so. She has his eyes, his nose, his colouring, his manner, while you are dark, like your mother.

Your sister is younger and shorter than you are, and her bedtime is half an hour earlier, but if you are to be permitted a biscuit before a meal-time, then so too must she. If you are to be given a sixpence, then so too must Lorraine. If it was your turn last time, then next time it has to be hers.

In all things but bedtime, in fact, you are to be equal – and expected to share – yet still you are supposed to look after her, because you are a big boy, and still she is regarded with more affection – for being a girl, and for being less inward, more open, than you are. And not just by your father, but by other men, too – for instance Ken Coatley next door, and Tom Balconer from over the road, who catches the bus into the Works with your father, and Sidney Goldman, who also works in the Works and drives a car and comes to your house to collect Annie, his wife, now that your mother has friends.

These and other men will tease your sister, joke with her – in time they will flirt with her, as they flirt with your mother – then laugh because she responds so cheerfully, so readily and innocently. You haven't her gift for cheerfulness, perhaps not even for innocence.

Your mother will disappear. Several afternoons each week she will take the bus into town, where she works as a cleaner in the various parts of the Civic Centre: the offices, cinema, theatre, ballroom, canteen and restaurant. Her shift lasts until five, sometimes five-thirty.

At seven and three quarters you are now in the Junior School, your sister still in the Infants, and while you wait for Mummy to come home on the bus it is Sally Clough who takes care of you, both you and Lorraine. She collects Lorraine from the school gates at three-forty, along with Andrew and Deborah, and allows you to make your own way to her house, since you are a big boy.

You let yourself in by her back door, and Sally pours you a beaker of squash and gives you a biscuit and asks you no questions about your day, since she is a housewife, and busy, and isn't your mother. You go to sit in her living room with your sister and Andrew and Deborah, who are watching the children's programmes on BBC1: *Jackanory, Animal Magic, Blue Peter, The Magic Roundabout.* These are the programmes you will remember, that everyone remembers.

Time for bed, Zebedee will say, and twirl about on his spring and twitch his moustache.

Time for tea, your mother will add, and wait for you to wake from the spell of the television.

She and Sally Clough will be smiling, standing in the doorway to Sally's kitchen. You will not have heard her come in.

In the evenings, too, your mother will often be gone, leaving your father in sole charge of you, if his shifts mean he must be at home, sitting smoking in his corner of the settee and drinking his cans of Long Life, the beer that is good for him. She goes to Keep Fit classes in the Community Centre next to St Christopher's. Some nights she and her friends – she calls them the girls – will be given tickets for shows at the Civic, if no one else wants them, and often she will be asked to waitress in the ballroom, if there is a function and she is available. Occasionally, too, she will babysit for Nadia, who has no husband and no longer lives with her parents: poor Nadia, who needs your mother to help her.

The reasons are explained to you. Her other absences, those nights when there is shouting, doors slamming, Mummy striding away in her heels, never will be explained, nor even mentioned.

Your mother will be gone from the house, and you will feel it; every time you will feel it. She will disappear – periodically this is what she will do – and so too, in a sense, will your sister, though she need not leave the house to be gone from your mind. For all the hours that you spend with Lorraine, siblings in these same rooms, sharing these furnishings, this wallpaper, this view to the garden, these parents, you will for long periods forget that she is there, and your older self, looking back at yourself, will frequently find that she is gone from the scene, a spectral presence in your memories, assumed by your recollections, but mostly absent, invisible.

It is in your elaborate games of make-believe that she becomes the most real to you, when you are able to invent her, as she invents you. *Just pretend you are Daddy. Just pretend I am Mummy.* Some days you are a doctor and she is a nurse. Some days you are a teacher and she is your pupil, or you are a shopkeeper and she is your customer. One day she is Dolores and you are called Ken, though your sister soon tires of that: so much talking is boring. But not every game requires a boy and a girl, a man and a woman. In one of your favourites you are both called Joe, the name of your father.

Let us play The Two Joes, says Peter.

Let us play.

Come on, Peter, says Lorraine.

Let us play The Two Joes.

And possibly your father is aware of this, and feels some pride or amusement, even affection towards you. Your older self – having achieved his age at last, the age at which he died – will want to believe so. Perhaps he lies upstairs in his bed and listens as he comes round from the day-long sleep that follows his night shift; perhaps your mother eavesdrops on your game and shares what she has heard with him when he returns from his day shift.

But the Joe of your imaginations is not a mere tradesman in the Works. He is someone who performs heroics such as you see in the other programmes you watch on TV: *Stingray, Thunderbirds, Batman, The Saint*. Then the settee will become a fire engine racing to rescue a stricken aeroplane at an airport as modern as your town centre, or a gargantuan green transporter like Thunderbird 2 – impossibly airborne – or a submarine that descends to the depths of the ocean, where the giant mechanical fish lies in wait for you, its Aquaphibian crew speaking in gurgles.

The games involve much energetic leaping to and from the settee, and rolling about on the floor, scrambling, hiding, springing back up again, and your sister is not always the junior, smaller

Joe; sometimes you will forget to remind her, and she will become the senior Joe, bossing her brother around.

You play harmoniously, mostly, and for as long as your mother is gone from the room she will be gone from your thoughts. She might be pegging out washing, making dinner, changing the bed-sheets. She won't be sleeping upstairs, or sitting in the kitchen with a can of beer and a cigarette, or reading the newspaper, as your father might do. It is possible she will have enough time to slip out to the mobile shop when it calls, or into a neighbour's house, and if she were to do this, you would not know. If Ken Coatley were to invite her next door to discuss her repayments, you would not know.

You do not know.

The afternoon you stab your sister in the eye you do not realise that your mother has left you to play in the house on your own.

The knife is the smallest in a set of five and has been missing since your father used it to peel an apple on Saturday, which is something he does expertly, removing the peel in one continuous spiral. He halved the bare apple for you to share with Lorraine, then ate the peel himself, holding it over his head and lowering it into his mouth as you stood by and watched him. He placed the paring knife on the arm of the settee and can't have noticed when it slipped down the side of the seat cushion. It has a brown Pukkawood handle that will not chip, crack or discolour. The blade is Sheffield steel. You notice the gleam of it when you stand on the settee.

Let's pretend the settee is a jeep, you say. Let's pretend we're in the jungle and I find this dagger over here in the bushes.

On Saturday you were watching *Daktari*, possibly *Tarzan*, and no doubt you have this in mind when you instruct your sister to be a crocodile and tell her to get down on the new blue Acrilan carpet. The weave is sinuous. On every map you have ever seen the rivers are depicted in blue. Your living room floor is a river.

You dive in after her, but your sister is tougher than you expect her to be, and as hard to subdue as a crocodile. Your ears become hot with the effort of holding her down as she writhes to get out from under you. At first you have her pinned to her belly, but then she thrashes, suddenly twists onto her back, and now she is facing you. The knife is between your teeth, then in your hand, and when you stab at her – this crocodile – you are careful only to pretend, even though she is making you mad. She is not playing how you want her to play; she won't do as you tell her to do. The point of the blade stops just short of her reptilian face. But your sister clutches your arm, no longer a crocodile, and the tussle now is for the knife, as in the films you have seen on TV of cowboys and Indians, goodies and baddies. She is a baddy, and she ought to submit to you. You will stab her to death if she does not submit to you. This is how you imagine it. You cannot know what Lorraine is imagining; nor do you anticipate the moment when she lets go of your arm and attempts to lift her head from the carpet.

There is a minuscule interval, the briefest duration, in which you notice the fineness of her hair, the filaments charged with static from the carpet, after which comes her scream. Something has happened.

The knife.

The cutting edge of the blade is not very fine, but the point is sharp and has nicked her left eyeball, just to the side of her pupil. You see a pearling of blood. Then there is another brief interval, a gap in which you notice nothing, and will remember nothing, before you find that both you and your sister are standing in the kitchen, looking for your mother, who is not there.

Rain dashes the windows. The light takes on a greenish hue. You smell scouring powder and see that Mummy has been cleaning the cooker again. The stove grids have been propped up to dry.

Your sister is screaming, one hand held over her eye, and the noise is piercing: it hurts your ears. You take her free hand and lead her through to the utility room – the shed; in your house it is known as 'the shed' – but Mummy is not there either. Nothing is out of place, and nothing is as it ought to be. The plastic ironing basket is empty. Your shoes are lined up in their pairs. Beneath the slope of the staircase your red and blue scooter is parked next to your sister's toy pram and her tricycle. All of this is as it ought to be, but your sister is screaming. You have stabbed her in the eye – you may have done it on purpose; you cannot be certain – and now you are frightened.

See Lorraine, Mother.

See Lorraine cry.

In the yellow-green light of the shed you hold Lorraine's hand and yell for your mother, who must be outside, and when at last she appears – the back door swinging inwards, her face stricken with worry – you notice Ken Coatley behind her, anxiously peering in from his side of the fence that divides your two gardens.

One flap of his shirt isn't tucked in to his trousers, and lifts in the breeze. He cringes because of the rain, and pushes his hands in his pockets.

Mummy gathers your sister into her arms, and tries to pry her hand from her eye, wincing because of the noise she is making. Let me see, sweetheart, she says, let Mummy have a look. Then she too is crying, her face twisted, aghast. Your sister's eyeball is red, entirely coated in blood. Mummy's skirt is unzipped, her slip showing white. You see this when she turns to Ken Coatley. She shouts for him to phone for an ambulance; she tells him to use the phone-box next to the Fine Fare.

Run, Ken, run! she shouts. Run fast!

Afterwards there is a long wait. Where are they? asks your mother. What can be keeping them?

There ought to be sirens. The rain continues to fall, slashing the window, flung by the wind. Occasionally a car comes near and drives on, its tyres hissing through the wet on the road. Your father will be waiting for the Works bus, if the message has reached him. The ambulance will be racing towards you. It has to come from the next town.

Exhausted by her screaming, your sister lies curled in Mummy's lap on the settee and whimpers. She sucks at her thumb, which she ought not to do, and you notice a purpling bruise on her thigh where her dress has rucked up. That too must be your fault; it must have come from your game. The knife has been placed on the mantelpiece for the ambulance men to examine, if that will help them, if they should ever arrive. Mummy holds a damp flannel to your sister's eye, and kisses the top of her head. You stand and stare at them. You think you should cover Lorraine's bruise, before anyone sees it, but you dare not go any nearer.

Mummy, is she going to be blind? you ask, and your mother says not, of course not, then looks past you and says, Thank you, Sally.

You feel a hand on your shoulder. Sally Clough is speaking kindly to you, suggesting you might like to come along to her house, where you can play with Andrew and Deborah. There's no need to cry, she says. Don't you worry, everything's going to be fine, you'll see.

It was only an accident, you say, and hope this isn't a lie.

Yes, I know, she replies.

I didn't mean it.

No, of course you didn't, she says.

Tearful, docile, you let yourself be led away. Ken Coatley steps aside to let you pass, concealing a cigarette behind his back. His shirt is tucked into his trousers. Sally Clough does not look at him, and he does not speak.

You will not see him again in your house. You cannot yet know this.

The following day it is Sidney Goldman – 'Uncle Sidney' – who brings your mother home from the hospital. He works a different shift to your father, clocking on as your father clocks off.

Your mother is now tearful, standing with Sally on the threshold to Sally's living room, while Uncle Sidney loiters in the kitchen behind them, jangling his car keys and looking around at the cupboards, which are identical to yours, though painted in blue. His trousers are grey Terylene, permanently pressed. His tee-shirt is Bri-Nylon, long-sleeved, soft-collared, a darker grey than his trousers, and there are two red stripes over his chest. He has a muscular chest.

When Uncle Sidney sees you watching him he pulls a funny face –boggle-eyed, pretending surprise – that forces you to smile even though you know you don't want to. You turn away from him. Your mother is discussing your sister with Sally, their voices hushed and serious, and anxiously you ask, Is she going to be blind now? Mummy, is Lorraine going to be blind? This seems to be what they are saying, up there above your head, where the adults converse. A surgeon will be operating to put a stitch or two in her eye, and the eye must be popped out of its socket for the operation to take place; this is the detail that most concerns you. Mummy, does that mean she's going to be blind? Mummy?

But she does not reply. It is Sally Clough who dips into your world, speaks to you directly. No, we don't think so, she says, and that is all you need know, for now; you take away this bit of news, you allow them to continue their conversation.

Andrew is colouring in. You sit and watch him, then reach for a crayon. The colour is 'magenta' and the stick is broken inside its paper sleeve. *Crayola.* You put it back down again. Moments later you are sick, throwing up on Andrew's colouring book, his mother's carpet, his lap.

You wake in your mother's bed and gaze at the ceiling, the blue-grey texture of darkness. Night-time is thicker than daytime. The texture is composed of millions of atoms, and they are tumbling towards you, falling out of the darkness. Atoms are the smallest things that exist, and they cannot hurt you, but still you cringe, sink into the pillows and close your eyes. You turn your head to one side and hear a bus moving off in the distance. You hear the raucous babble on board, the passengers yelling and laughing, a bell repeatedly ringing. But these sounds are too loud; they must be inside your head.

You open one eye and stare at the curtains. The clack of heels on the pavement will be your mother approaching. You lie still and listen, you strain to be certain. The sound of her stilettos grows larger, swells into the bedroom, and you realise you must be mistaken: the shape of the sounds is all wrong. As they continue on past your house, gradually recede into the distance, you ask yourself anxiously what becomes of these footsteps once they've been heard; where do they go to? Is this something you know?

Every sound falls away into silence, and is replaced by the next sound. The moments slip away, the footsteps, the sounds. Somewhere in the future, in another part of the estate, the sound of those heels will be approaching. Somewhere in the past, the sounds will have gone.

You are becoming the past, and the sounds are now like a whisper, quieter than a whisper. It is inside your head. You sit up in the bed before you are sick. You clamp your hands to your ears.

The light comes on, Mummy hurries into the bedroom. What is it? she says; why are you screaming?

Ω

Later, possibly earlier, you are woken by voices. It is morning. There is a blue plastic bucket at the side of the bed. The bucket smells of the cupboard under the sink.

You pad out to the landing and find a stranger, a black man, in a heavy grey overcoat. He is talking to your father. There has never been a black man in your house before, and you wonder if this is something your father is also surprised by, if in fact he is angry and asking him to leave.

Your mother once ran away with a black man. Perhaps this is the man. He is much taller than your father, as tall as the ceiling, and in one large hand he grips the handle of a brown leather bag; in the other he pinches a king-sized cigarette. His shoes are highly polished, his pin-stripe trousers have turn-ups. Neither this man nor your father pays you any attention, and you notice that your bedroom door is a little way open. The curtains are closed. Mummy must be in there in the dark. You can see the atoms vibrating.

What's the matter with Mummy? you ask. Is Mummy poorly again?

But though they glance round at you, neither man answers. Your father solemnly follows the black man downstairs. You stand at the top of the staircase and watch them shake hands, as men do, first clamping their cigarettes between their lips. When the stranger touches your father on his shoulder he seems even taller, your father much smaller, as small as a child. Your father opens the front door for him, quietly shuts it behind him.

Back to bed, he says then, growing larger as he comes up the stairs. Never you mind now, just you get back into bed.

৯৻

Later your mother will confirm that a doctor has been, and no, she does not think he was a black man, and he didn't come to see her, because she was in the hospital, visiting your sister.

This time you are the one who is poorly. The doctor has prescribed two bottles of medicine, oddly flavoured syrups, one pink and one white. You allow the syrups to be tipped into your mouth. You sink back to the pillows, sink back into sleep, and picture a pavement, a soldier, a tree. The pavement is perfectly smooth, a grey so pale it is almost white. It passes beneath the branches of the tree, a tree so shiny and sharp it must be fashioned from steel. You are looking down from a window, your perspective some way over the tree, when along the pale pavement comes the soldier. He is dressed in khaki green. The fabric is smooth and synthetic, permanently pressed. It is Terylene, possibly that. The backdrop is blank; the soldier's expression is blank. He might be blind. His footsteps make no sound. As he passes under the tree he tilts his face towards you. Repeatedly he passes under the tree, which is a fruit tree. Must it be an apple tree? There is a single fruit, a pear. The soldier looks up at you. Sightlessly he sees you, and then you are falling, tumbling towards him, which is when you wake, afraid you might be sick again.

For seven days and nights you remain in your parents' bed, taking your medicines, the mop bucket beside you, your fever subsiding, the sheets becoming fustier, until finally your mother says you must go back to your own bed. Daddy thinks you have had long enough to get better; it is his turn now to sleep next to Mummy.

And it is often this way, your father's wishes communicated by your mother in a voice that is both kindly and stern: Lorraine, she explains, will be coming home soon from the hospital, and there is no need for you to keep having nightmares, to keep complaining that you are unwell.

All right, you say.

A good boy, you do as you are told. Barefoot in your pyjamas, you stand to one side as she begins to strip down her bed, then you turn and walk through to your own bedroom, which smells sourly of the nights your father has slept there.

You sit on the edge of your mattress, re-acquaint yourself with the appearance of things. The sun dims. Streaks of rain slash the window. You sit and look at the roofs of the houses behind, the clouds overhead. Chicken soup? asks Mummy, and you nod. It must be dinner-time. She is clutching a bundle of sheets to her tummy. She tells you to put on some clean clothes, bring your pyjamas downstairs for the wash.

Your sister is never as sickly as you are. Already, in 1967, when you are seven and she is five, you have shared in all the usual contagions of childhood – mumps, chicken pox, measles, innumerable colds – and it has entered the lore of your family that your sister does not know how to be poorly. You have heard your father saying those words: Oh, this one doesn't know how to be poorly. Which is, it seems, another mark in her favour, though your mother, you realise, is exasperated by her refusal to rest, her impatience to be up and about.

Conveyed home from the hospital in Uncle Sidney's pale blue Cortina, she smells of the ward, and wears a lumpy lint dressing over her left eye, and a transparent patch over the dressing. The white elasticated strap for the patch cuts into her hair, causing it to curl out at odd angles, and there is a circular Elastoplast on the back of her hand. This is where the needle went in, she tells you. It put me to sleep, I had an operation.

You're skinny, you remark, and notice, too, that her lips are as pale as her face, and dry. She has been to the hospital and had an operation, and yet still – the moment Uncle Sidney beeps his horn and drives off – she begins an inspection of the house, a headlong tour of her toys. She takes her tricycle on a circuit of the living room, then drags out her box of teddies and dolls from under the sideboard and lines them up on the settee, then disappears upstairs and carries down from her bedroom a sloping pile of jigsaws and games that holds her attention for a matter of minutes.

Amused, your father watches over her, while your mother tidies the mess she is making. Envious, you kneel on the fireside rug and sort through the gifts she's been given.

There are so many things, enough to fill the kitbag your father has retrieved from the attic. It seems Lorraine has been rewarded in hospital with an additional birthday, for there are cards and colouring books, comics and crayons, sweeties and bottles of squash. You extract a Sindy doll, an air hostess with a glistening helmet of blond nylon hair on which is perched a blue BOAC cap, and a game called Frustration, the rattling box depicting another family of four, all of them laughing, their faces eager, delighted: father, mother, their two children. POP-O-MATIC, says an arrow on the lid.

Can we play this? you ask, and tilt the picture to show to your mother.

No, she says, and snatches a bottle of Lucozade from the rug. Your father follows her into the kitchen, his hand reaching for her bottom, and she slaps him away. She is angry, it seems; you cannot know why. But your father is cheerful. For now, he is smiling.

Lorraine has come home, and though in the weeks to come your mother will have several long murmurous conversations with Sally Clough in your living room, and will often be tearful, and your sister will return several more times to the hospital, and there will be eye-drops and patches, and visits to an optician in town, soon enough it will be confirmed that her vision is fine. She will be able to see from the eye that you stabbed. You won't have ruptured the globe; her eyeball won't have deflated. But the pupil will be forever misshapen, making her appear at first glance to have a boss eye, or even a fake one. Other children will tease her. She will never be sickly, but you will have spoiled her. Perhaps you did this on purpose; that thought will never leave you. Perhaps you have made her less pretty. For now, you won't be able to tell, though she will remain her father's favourite, of that you will be certain – and you will be glad; in time you will come to be glad about that.

1968

it is none of your business

I T I S 1968, and at this time, in your town, fewer than one in
five households has a motor car, though the national figure is
nearer one in two. Fewer than one in four homes has a telephone,
against a national figure of two in every three. But the figure for
most other amenities is higher than the average: more refrigerators,
washing machines, vacuum cleaners, radiograms, televisions. And
of course for the populace, who have come to escape the conges-
tion and squalor of the great conurbations, the environmental
amenities are equally plentiful, at least to the west of the Works:
fresh air and spacious horizons, well-built homes with decent-sized
gardens in healthful, well-planted surroundings.

Yours is a town of rented accommodation but few private
landlords, full employment but little self-employment. The Works
is the principal employer, and almost all of the housing is owned
by the Development Corporation, some by the Council. Every

house comes with a handbook. One day you will read it. Pets are permitted. Alterations, additions and installations are not, though tenants are invited to treat their homes as if they were their own. They are advised to redecorate every five years, and urged to be house-proud and to keep their gardens tidy; they are challenged to be the envy of their neighbours. And many do try, including your parents.

At this time, in your town, there are more young married couples and more young children, and fewer of the middle-aged and the elderly, than may be found in many other, more established towns. These couples are busy home-making, and determined to prosper. A documentary film has been made about them, a cinema newsreel that you have yet to see, which shows them congregating in a community hall to listen to a lecture. A planner points to maps, drawings and diagrams. In their winter coats and hats and scarves, the audience is attentive, appreciative, and applauds at the end. They have a pioneering spirit and optimistic outlook that means they are at ease in the company of strangers. They are willing users of public transport. They hail each other across the shared public spaces. Almost all of them belong to the working or artisanal class.

The managerial and entrepreneurial middle class live in the surrounding villages, which was not part of the plan, and is re-grettable, since your town was intended to mark a victory for the rational, the balanced and the purposeful; it was designed to run with the ease of a piece of precision machinery, providing oppor-tunities for a full life, economic and social, in order to produce a new type of citizen, freed from the bane of class segregation. You are supposed to become that new type of citizen: self-respecting, dignified, and possessed of a sense of civic belonging, though of course you won't know this. You are just eight years old.

You are eight in 1968, and until you move up to second year Juniors you will remain in One Red: a mere first year, though big enough now to be sent out on errands, in a neighbourhood where everyone knows everyone, in a town where it is safe for children to wander. You are big enough now to run and fetch your father's cigarettes from the precinct. He smokes forty, fifty, sixty cigarettes every day, and really he ought to give up. Your mother is tired of telling him. He can kill himself if he wants to, but she is sick of the sound of him coughing, and sick of the smell of him, too.

She does not want him near her.

You fetch the pad of blue Basildon Bond from the drawer in the sideboard. Your father writes with a black fibre-tipped pen, issued by the Works, which he keeps clipped to the inside pocket of his donkey jacket. You know this because you have been spying, though that is not a word you would use; you would say looking. The jacket is grimy and stinks of the Works and hangs from a peg in the shed, the gas and electricity meters above it.

He sits at the yellow-topped table in the kitchen, and you stand and watch as he dates and carefully composes the letter. He is proud of his penmanship, his tidy calligraphy:

Dear Sir or Madam,
    I am writing to request that you sell my son 60 Embassy
Tipped cigarettes. I have enclosed a pound note and I would

be grateful if you would give him the correct change.
Yours faithfully.

His signature is illegible, but just as neatly inscribed. He traces out the curlicues, then adds a full-stop as if tapping in a rivet. He flattens the banknote and folds the letter over it, then folds it again, pressing the creases as sharp as the line in his trousers. He is going somewhere important – Never you mind where – and will be staying overnight. He has packed his army kitbag. He is wearing a black knitted tie.

Don't lose it, he warns you.

Can I get some sweets?

Don't drop the change either.

Dad, can I?

Sixpence. That's all.

You run most of the way, tightly gripping his note. The precinct means sweets; you can choose them yourself. But there is something else too, something like a secret; you sense it each time you go there.

The shops are arranged as two parades, aligned at right angles to each other. The passage between them leads to a rubble-strewn field of tussocky grass, awaiting development. One parade is longer than the other – five shops and three shops, you have counted them. A continuous canopy in white concrete unifies the shopfronts and creates an impression of architectural harmony. It affords protection to pedestrians in bad weather, shade for the window displays on sunnier days. It shelters the passageway.

Above the shorter of the two parades rises the tallest building in your estate, a block of flats four storeys high that looks down on an expanse of paving slabs in which are dispersed three slender trees in protective cages, three slatted benches, four metal bins.

You leap onto the first of the benches, balance on the end of it. Your shadow is small, a fat little fellow. You look around at the shops, this familiar scene, and you are struck by the thought that you are observing a memory, something you will later come to remember. The Spastics Society girl waits outside the Fine Fare; she will always be waiting. Carole Coatley serves inside the bakers, where you must never go. The door to the greengrocer's releases a smell of soil and carrots and leaves, and all is expectancy, everything still. Nothing here is any older than you are, and nothing will ever be this modern again.

To your older self, recalling this moment, the precinct will resemble a planner's scale model, an architect's drawing. But the future it promises will never arrive, and may already have gone. In a few more years the concrete will begin to discolour; chunks will fall from the canopy. The paintwork on the shop-fronts will blister. The bins will begin to corrode, and will be emptied less often, an attraction for flies in the heat. The saplings will perish, despite their cages. Stripped by boys of their bark, they will be skeletal even in summer, and when eventually the precinct is re-contoured to make space for a car-park the trees will be taken away, along with the benches.

By then the passageway will have begun to smell pissy. A gathering place for teenagers – smoking and spitting – it will mark the boundary to a new territory, an infill estate of flat-roofed, high-density dwellings, a warren of alleyways, courtyards and culs-de-sac, possessing no through-road, and no centre. Graffiti will appear. The shops will be secured with metal shutters at night. Some shutters will remain lowered all day. Some will remain lowered for years.

History cannot be predicted. The Lingwood Road precinct, intended to mark a break with the past, will come to stand for a different past, a different future. But none of this – the inevitability of this – can yet be known to you. Perhaps this is its secret.

You don't go into the Fine Fare, where there are aisles of goods and trolleys to fill and no one to guide you. In the Fine Fare the assistants sit tight at the tills, and the sweets are in wrappers on shelves, the kind you see everywhere. Instead you jump from your bench and charge over the precinct to Grieve's, the post office and general store, where nothing may be handled before it is bought. Each item in turn must be requested from one of the assistants and taken down from the shelves at the back of the shop. Mr Grieve wears a white shop-coat and operates the ham slicer; Mrs Grieve peers out from the enclosure of the post office counter. The lady assistants wear brown nylon aprons, and have moveable steps to reach the highest of the shelves, and whenever you present them with a note from your father they will smile and confer. Isn't that lovely? they will say; what lovely handwriting!

Twenty Embassy Tipped costs 3/10d, which makes 11/6d for sixty, and you are given a sixpence in your change. Then you are in charge; the tanner is yours.

At the sweetie counter, on any other day, one of the ladies

will wait on your instructions and patiently fill a paper bag with a selection of sweets priced in ha'pennies and pennies. But not today. Today you ask for two packets of Barratt's *Thunderbirds* Sweet Cigarettes, since each pack of ten costs 3d and contains a collectable card. Andrew Clough has the full set, pasted into an album. The glue smells of fish.

You get a number 23, Jeff Tracy's house, and a number 31, Lady Penelope's drawing room. Neither is an action shot, or one of the *Thunderbirds* craft, and in your disappointment you eat four sticks at once, a squeaky mush in your mouth, and drop the cards in one of the bins in the precinct, where you notice an Embassy coupon, still in its box. You slip the coupon in your pocket, then inspect each of the other bins and retrieve three more of them, all fives. It cannot be stealing to take them.

Every pack of twenty Embassy contains a sky-blue coupon worth five points; every pack of ten contains a coupon worth two. *Embassy – The Best in Smoking* declare the coupons, above an address in Glasgow for obtaining a catalogue. Your father keeps his coupons on a shelf in his wardrobe, neatly stacked in blocks secured with rubber bands. The catalogue is slim, and isn't for children. Whenever you ask what he is saving for, he says an iron lung.

No, but really? you press him.

Really, he says.

As you stroll home now from the precinct, a red-tipped candy stick held between the fingers of your right hand, your father's Embassys in your left hand – a mini-man, a smoker – you scour the kerbs and shrubberies for more discarded coupons. Some are discoloured, some grubby with dirt, and each time you reach for one you clamp the sweetie cigarette in your lips. You pinch your eyes against the smoke, exhale from the side of your mouth. You are only pretending.

Dad, look! you call as you come into the house; I found you some coupons!

But if he is grateful he does not reveal it. You have nearly made him late with your dawdling. A black cab has drawn up at the kerb, and as your father hurries from the house you notice the shine on his shoes, as bright as the cellophane wrap he tears from the cigarettes and drops to the pavement. He is carrying his best suit on a hanger, sheathed in a Sketchley's green wrapper. He is going to Glasgow to bury his mother, though this is not yet something you know. No one has told you. It is none of your business.

Mummy says you must remember what to buy. She will not write it down for you. Her handwriting is clumsy, full of capitals, spelling mistakes, letters turned back-to-front – which is one more difference between them. Her handwriting is worse even than Lorraine's.

You must remember the list, and take your sister too, and be careful at the roads. In Grieve's you are to ask one of the ladies to pack the shopping bag for you, and put Mummy's change in the purse. You and Lorraine can have one penny each to spend on sweeties, no more. Only two pennies. Do you remember what you have to ask for? Peter, can you say it?

You repeat the list aloud for her, then over and over as you climb Witton Way and descend Seething Green, traverse the swing park and begin the ascent of Horsford Avenue, you whisper the sing-song sound of the words to yourself: *a pint of milk, a packet of tea,*

*a thin-sliced loaf and four ounces of ham please . . . a pint of milk,
a packet of tea, a thin-sliced loaf and four ounces of ham please . . .*

But soon your mouth starts to taste coppery, and the words become mere shapes in your mouth, meaningless plosives, sibilants, aspirates, a sound like panic inside your head. Lorraine is dawdling ever further behind you, amiably chatting to herself, carefully gesticulating, her face kindly but serious, as if she were an adult explaining this errand to a child just like herself.

The Lingwood Road precinct is just over the road, suddenly bright in a moment of sunshine. Shadows appear: lacy trees and sharp-angled buildings, your squat shape on the pavement. You have to cross at the zebra. A car has stopped for you. The letters on the registration plate spell TUB. The man at the wheel gestures through the glare on his windscreen. But Lorraine first needs to catch up, and you can't be sure what you have come for: *a pint of tea, a packet of milk . . .*

In your confusion you think you may have dropped your mother's purse. You look back the way you have come – at the mica glinting in the pavement, at the shadowy verges – but if you dropped anything your sister would surely have seen it, and anyway, of course, the purse will be zipped inside the shopping bag that is tucked under your arm. The bag is maroon vinyl, the handles hooped over your shoulder. The purse is green leatherette and contains a ten shilling note.

The car beeps its horn, a long note of annoyance as it pulls away from the crossing. Your sister meanders towards you. Come on, you say, we have to go back to Mum.

I don't want to.

Come on, you have to!

But I want to go to the shops.

Come *on!*

The cloud returns, the shadows recede. You cannot wait for her.

Holding tight to the shopping bag, you set off at a run down Horsford Avenue, the paving slabs streaking under your plimsoles. You sprint across the swing park, then pound up the playing field, feeling the weight of the rise in your legs, the bumps and divots in the grass. You slow near the top to gather your breath. You pace backwards through the metal goalposts and scan the scene for Lorraine.

She is standing small in the swing park, her arms truculently crossed on her tummy. She is staring straight back up at you. She is squinting because of the sun.

There is no time; you must leave her. You turn and keep running, and in moments you are bursting through the back door. But your mother is not where you expected her to be, not as you left her, kneeling in the kitchen in her headscarf and pinny, about to start cleaning the cooker. The oven door is open, a plastic bucket of water beside it, a skim of grey froth on the surface.

Mum!

At this age your mother can sometimes be Mum; your father is Dad.

You find her in the living room, staring out at your garden. She is standing in the corner where the birdcage once stood. Bars of sunlight slice across her from the blinds, and she is smoking a cigarette, her right elbow cupped in her left hand, the cigarette held between two slender fingertips, inches from her lips. She does not smoke. She says it is disgusting.

Why are you smoking? you say.

She does not hear you.

Mummy? Why are you smoking?

Her head turns, as if the sound of you has taken some seconds to reach her. She contemplates the fact that you are there, standing in the doorway to the kitchen. You were quick, she says then, her voice catching, thick in her throat.

I forgot what things you said to get. Why are you smoking? It's disgusting.

My nerves. It is for my nerves. What did you forget?

What to buy. Mum, can you write it down for me?

She glances at the shopping bag beneath your arm, seeming then to grasp its significance. She nods and takes a long inhalation, then picks up a glass from the window ledge. Your mum has been drinking. She empties the glass and wanders into the kitchen, extinguishes the cigarette in the sink and drops it in the pedal bin. Smoke seeps from her nose and her mouth. She hesitates, then tears the flap from a cereal packet, and as she casts about for a pen she realises that Lorraine is not with you.

Where is Lorraine? she asks, and when you don't answer she steps through to the shed, looks quickly around. The door to the garden is open. She goes out, calls Lorraine's name, comes back inside.

She wouldn't hurry up, you complain. She never does what I tell her to. Mum, can you write it down for me?

Write what!

The shopping things.

But Peter, where is she? Where is Lorraine?

Your mother's breath is sour from the cigarette, sweet from the alcohol. Her face is suddenly inches from yours. Her eyes are swollen, red-rimmed, hugely magnified by her spectacles. The bruise on her cheekbone, which had almost gone away, shows again through her make-up. She grips you tightly at the top of your arms.

Where is your sister? she shouts. *Where is Lorraine?* But she is making you cry, not letting you answer. Nothing is still because she is shaking you, and when she lets go it's as if she has pushed you. The walls seem to slide, but you don't fall down; stunned, you stop crying.

Hastily she pulls off her pinny, drops it on the table. Your father will kill you, she shouts then, and kicks off her slippers. He will kill you, I swear. And this time I will let him!

Her slingbacks are next to the litter bin, the heels and toes scuffed, the white leather cracked. In her hurry she can't get the straps over her heels and gives a cry of exasperation, almost a scream.

Mummy, you say then. Mum!

Your sister has come back after all. She is looking in from the doorstep, clammy from running.

Where have you been! yells your mother. *Where have you been?* Then plaintively, sobbing, her fingers in her hair: Where have you been, Lorraine?

Your sister stares up at her quizzically. Her mouth becomes taut, her chin starts to tremble, then she too starts to cry. But you are a big boy. You take a step nearer your mother. You reach out a hand. At arm's length you comfort her; consolingly you stroke the sleeve of her cardigan.

There, there, you say to your mother.

Another day, it must be soon after. You are alone in the house. Your mother has gone to the doctor's; perhaps he can help her. She has taken your sister, since you cannot be trusted to take care of her. Your father has come back from Glasgow. He has gone back to work and you have closed your bedroom door and opened his wardrobe. It smells of varnished wood, leather and polish, dry laundered fabric. It smells of your father, the mystery of him.

His clothes hang from a thin metal rail, as though for inspection: his shirts and trousers, his good jacket, his best and second-best suits and two coats, his braces, his ties. Most of the shirts are white; most of the trousers are grey. Some are yet to be worn. He has two pairs of slacks in ICI polyester-fibre that need never be ironed. The jacket is Harris tweed, with a lining of bronze rayon satin and buttons like tiny half-footballs. One of the coats is double-breasted suedette in dark fawn, the other is grey Gannex. You have been here before, examined the labels, felt around in the pockets.

Item by item, you lay his clothes on your bed and select a tie, a white shirt, a pair of grey trousers. You try on your father for size. You roll up his sleeves, the hem of the trousers. You clip on some braces. You step into a pair of his shoes.

Your white wicker chair creaks as you climb onto it. If you raise yourself on tiptoe you will be able to reach the back of the shelf, but for now you are not touching, only looking. Everything is tidy: boxed or stacked, squarely aligned. Here are his coupons, saved up for the future. And here are his gift-sets, his Old Spice and Brylcreem, his shoe-shine kit and his shaver, still in its box.

Carefully you take out these items and place them on your windowsill. Then you add a maroon paisley-pattern scarf, and a long slim box containing three 'bobtail' neck-ties, the colours autumnal: *Woodland Shades*. You gave these to him last Christmas; you chose them from the catalogue. Smashing, he said, and put them aside. The box has never been opened.

Later you will need to replace everything just as you found it, but further back there are treasures. You reach in for the boxes containing his medals, which are only for looking at, not for playing with. He received them for good conduct, long service, efficiency. That is all. You place the boxes beside the Elastoplast tin that contains his two shrivelled pieces of cartilage, preserved in a fold of cream-coloured bandage. They came from his knee, and you have also seen them before; he has allowed you to touch them.

All the rest is new to you. Here is a Ronson *Veraflame* cigarette lighter, sleek and gold in a velvet-lined case, and a Parker *65 Flighter* fountain pen in brushed stainless steel. And here is a wristwatch – *Smiths Empire Shockproof 5 Jewels* – with gold numerals and a gold expandable bracelet. How often has your father complained he could use a new watch? If you were to position it nearer the front, would he be puzzled not to have noticed it sooner, and pleased to have found it? You picture him smiling, then picture him angry. These are his things and you should not be touching them. They are none of your business. But still, you reach in for the largest item, a brown leatherette file. Cautiously you climb down from the chair in his oversized shoes and sit on the edge of your mattress.

The file unzips around three sides and contains papers, certificates, a football programme, some magazines. It may be adrenaline that causes the sensation of plunging, of having been dropped. You look to your bedroom door, listen to the sounds of the house, the pulse in your ears. Everything is just as it was. The light outside is lemony; perhaps it will rain. You open one of the magazines.

Of course you have seen your mother in her underwear, and without any clothes on. You have stared down at her as she soaks in the bath, her brow moist with sweat, her breasts floating at the surface. Sometimes she will spread out a flannel to cover her privates, her fuzz of black hair. And though you know what she is concealing – you have seen her climb out of the bath – you don't yet have a name for it. In your mind it is still her 'dolores', her 'dolly'.

Now you absorb this new information: the differently shaped breasts, the variety of sizes – plump and pointed, saggy and small – and the fleshiness of the women's private parts, the wetness and folds, the pinkness of the skin inside the skin, the wiry hair that surrounds it. There are men in these pictures too, their faces expressionless. A man's peter is also a willy. These men's willies are poking straight out. You look at the women with their mouths around the men's willies, and the men with their willies going inside the women. None of these people seems happy. The men have moustaches. All the writing is foreign.

You close the magazine before you get to the end; you swallow in case you are sick. The other magazines are the same: so many pictures of grown-ups without any clothes on, so many close-ups of privates. If you showed them to your mother, would you be in trouble, or would your father? You should not be looking. He ought not to have left them here for you to find them.

Your hands have become damp; you can feel the tackiness in your fingers as you pick up the programme. It is England versus West Germany, the World Championship Jules Rimet Cup final at the Empire Stadium, Wembley, on Saturday July 30 1966, price 2/6. Your father has never once showed this to you, never even mentioned he owns it. This too is a secret, but boys are interested in football and he ought to have shared it. Also, your father is Scottish, and you are English; you were born in this house. The programme should be yours instead of his. If you were to keep it, would he even realise? If you were to hide it somewhere in this room, would that be stealing?

You look around at his things, spread out on your bed, the floor, his chest of drawers. You look at yourself in your mirror, dressed as your father. You stare at the emptied shell of his wardrobe, you stare for a long time, then you pick up his magazines. Your dad is disgusting, and your mother should know this.

In their bedroom you open your arms, watch as his magazines fall to her pillow. Then you return to his wardrobe and begin to replace each of his things, item by item, exactly as he would want them. You are meticulous. You are eight and three quarters, and just as tidy as he is.

1969

acres of ground for acres of pleasure

A TYPICAL DWELLING on the Bawdeswell estate has 960 square feet of internal floor space. Your parents' bedroom measures eleven feet six inches by eleven feet three, and now contains two beds, twin singles delivered from Smarts, the Complete Home Furnishers in town. The beds are six feet three inches long and two feet eleven inches wide. The gap between them is two feet exactly. The gap between your parents is wider. Even at this age, you are able to see that.

Your house is twenty-two feet deep and has a frontage twenty-four feet across, including the passage to the left of the house, which is three feet ten inches wide and leads through to the garden. The gate is glossed white, and is three feet two inches high. The garden is spartan, rectangular, almost twice as long as it is wide: forty-five feet.

These are the dimensions of new town family life, and like

all the gardens in your neighbourhood, your private measure of land is enclosed by a chain-link fence, a diamond-shaped mesh that is just too high for you to hurdle. You have tried. Aged nine, you are small for your age – four feet two inches tall – but you are physically active. You are forever sprinting, hurdling, climbing.

A narrow pathway bisects the garden, a lumpy lawn to either side of it. Your mother's washing line stretches the length of the pathway, a metal pole half-way down it. The pole is six feet two inches tall, with narrow cleats at the top, around which the rope has been wound.

It is spring or early summer – let us settle on spring – and one afternoon as your sister digs for worms in the flower bed, and your mother stands at the sink in the kitchen, and your father sits smoking in the airless dark of the living room, and Peggy kneels with Bill in their alpine rock garden, and Mr Sarrison at number 84 forces a rattling lawn-mower back and forth on his lawn, you shimmy up the pole and grip the ends of the cleats.

You use these as your handles and attempt to stay at the top of the pole for as long as you can, for as long as there is strength in your arms. It is a challenge to yourself, and of course you keep slipping, but each time you slip back a fraction you tug yourself up again, clamping your thighs to the pole. You perform this motion repeatedly – slipping and clamping, clamping and slipping – and in this way you discover how to pleasure yourself, fully on view to your parents, your sister, the neighbours.

No one can know what you are experiencing. Your interior life is invisible; your thoughts and feelings cannot be seen.

Your peter is softly pressed to the pole, sliding against it; your perineum too. The tickling sensation begins in your privates and spreads up to your belly and back to your bottom. It resembles the thrill of reaching the top of the arc on a swing in the swing-park, then plunging back down again. It is like the feeling as you speed over a humpback bridge in Uncle Sidney's Cortina, everyone squealing. But there is no end to it. Your nose is pressed to the cold blunt smell of the pole; your arms are beginning to ache. Yet the sensation continues, and it makes your mouth water, also your eyes, and when your father appears at the living room window, grimly inhaling the last of a cigarette, you tighten your grip.

Eventually you must fall, but you are seeing how long you can stay at the top of the pole, how long you can bear it. Perhaps he will be proud of you, the strength in your arms.

You are nine, and the pursuit of this sensation becomes for a while a compulsion.

There is also the pole at the front of your house, which supports the concrete canopy over the porch, and the metal goalposts on Seething Green, and the washing-line poles in the drying court behind the flats on Ringland Road, where you challenge Andrew Clough to see who can remain aloft for the longest, and immediately lose interest when he grunts and confesses, My willy is tickling.

Mine isn't, you say, sliding down, and wait for him to descend. He tugs out the waistband of his shorts, using both thumbs, and peers in at his privates. He grins at you stupidly.

I've got to go home now, you say, and set off at a sprint. You leave him behind, for this must be your secret. No one must know what you are experiencing; your thoughts and feelings must not be shared.

Yet still you persist. In Welborne Walk there is a lamppost half-way down the pavement, a creosoted fence alongside it. By climbing onto the fence you can elevate yourself above the lower, fatter part of the lamppost, then begin shimmying up, all the way to the top, from where you can see into every back garden in your row of houses, and those beyond and behind, far into the distance.

Of course you can also be seen by every one of your neighbours. You are now visible from dozens of windows, clinging to the top of the lamppost, your arms embracing the lantern, your thighs clamping and slipping as you make yourself delirious eighteen feet from the ground.

A pale green car passes beneath you, a growling Volkswagen Beetle. A young man and woman pause at the end of the street and look up at you, laughing. Then your mother appears in your garden. She shouts at you to come down from there, come down at once, or you will fall and break your neck. She is wearing white mules, a scarf in her hair, paisley-print slacks in orange and turquoise. Your life is being lived in the Sixties – you don't yet know that it is – and today is a coffee morning.

Come inside now! she calls to you.

You slide down the pole, as far as the fence, then jump to the pavement. You land in a crouching position, your knees bent, fingers touching the paving slab. It is the start of a race. You count backwards from five, then *go!*

The kitchen is laid with plates of the foreign foods that you and your father won't eat – the pastries and dips and bowls of cold pasta that have garlic in them, olive oil, tomato paste, anchovies. But she is making ordinary sandwiches, too: egg and tomato, cheese and spring onion. The best cups sit in their saucers. The kettle is beginning to bubble. Some of the women have already arrived: you hear Annie Goldman laughing in the living room, and watch as your mother arranges the sandwiches. She speaks to you quietly. Her fingers are shaking.

You must not climb the lamppost, Peter. It is very dangerous.

Not really, you object.

Or this pole in the garden, she says; not any more. The neighbours can see what you are doing. Do you understand me?

I was counting how many seconds I could stay at the top.

I know, she says, and looks at you closely. But you must not do it. Okay? It is wrong, Peter. Everyone can see you. Your father has seen you. Do you understand me?

She waits, and reluctantly you nod, though there are poles in every swing-park, placed there for children to climb on. Children are meant to be active, especially boys, and you were just being active, seeing how long you could stay at the top of the pole. If your mother can still see inside you, this is the thought that she will find there.

Here, she says then, and gives you a sandwich. Go and play now. Go and play with your friends.

Many years in the future you will confirm the names of the streets in your neighbourhood with the aid of a street map, which will reveal surprising connections, parts continuous with other parts, displaced by your memory, but there will be no map or almanac to help you remember the people who live in the houses, or the boys that you play with, whose names will fade with their faces, leaving barely any impression, despite the hours that you spend in their company, exploring and stalking, fighting, hiding, building dens. You will have no choice but to invent them.

Don't go far, your mother will tell you; be careful crossing the roads.

And for now you are careful, and stay within the bounds of your estate, which is two thirds of a mile in length, half a mile wide, and contains a variety of plantings maintained by the Corporation to provide a seasonally changing environment, a pleasing visual amenity.

At the curve in your street, for example, there is a plantation of bushes and trees, not much older than you are, through which you and the other boys will forge pathways and build hide-outs and learn that crab apples are inedible and the seeds in rose-hip pods will cause itches.

Just round in Welborne Walk there's a smaller plantation where you and Andrew Clough will secrete yourselves on your bellies, having laid a trap to capture a sparrow – a cardboard box, the lid propped up on a stick, a length of wool tied to the base of the stick. A trail of breadcrumbs is your bait. Time will pass. Shadows will lengthen. No birds will be tempted.

In Postwick Court the bushes provide a low canopy beneath which a boy called Lenny will demonstrate how to make smoke signals, first filling a bottle half-way with dry soil, then covering its mouth with one hand and shaking it vigorously before thumping it twice on the ground and momentarily lifting his hand to release a haze of brown dust: the smoke.

Wherever you go there will be dog shit, on every pavement and field, in the bushes, grass verges, and all over Seething Green, where you and Brendan O'Neil will compete to be killed, first nominating the weapon with which you are to be shot – arrow, machine gun, torpedo – then rushing headlong towards it, the winner being the one who dies the most spectacularly, aping the westerns and war films that you watch on the television, until Brendan slides through a lump of soft excrement and has to go home to get cleaned.

Later he will smell of Dettol, which is harmless to everything but germs. The smear in the grass will remain until the next time it rains.

On Seething Green you will also play football, accompanying yourself with a commentary in the style of Hugh Johns on the television, though better than any field is the square of municipal garages at the top of Witton Way, where the ball will skid off the rough concrete, picking up scuffs and striations, bits of grit embedded in the plastic, and crash repeatedly into the coloured metal doors, causing such a racket that Mrs Morgan will eventually appear in her housecoat and slippers to shoo you away. She knows your name and where you live; she will be speaking to your mother, and you needn't think you can cheek her.

These are some of the things you will come to remember, that you will insist on remembering, though not all of your friends at this time will be boys, since there is also Linda Goldman, who will come with you on holiday and remain in your memory, your first friend who is a girl, perhaps your first girlfriend.

Your chalet on holiday has a bunk-bed. This is the first thing you notice as you come through the door, and no doubt you will want to take the top tier, being a boy, and the oldest, and so fond of high places.

No, Lorraine can have it, you say, I don't mind.

Your sister squints up at your father, hardly daring to smile. He places his hand on her head, her shining brown hair.

You are sure? asks your mother.

You consider your options, then nod. She can if she wants to, you say.

Yes! cries Lorraine, and clambers straight up the ladder and flops onto the mattress. Immediately she pretends to fall fast asleep, her hands pressed together as if in prayer, pillowing her face.

Okay then, sighs Mum. That is decided. If you change your mind, it is too bad.

I won't, you say, and crawl onto your mattress.

Me neither, says your sister.

The word *Butlin's* is emblazoned in red on the candlewick coverlet. Beside you and behind you the walls are smoothly painted in peach. The upper bunk rests on a frame of diagonal wires, the mattress bulging through the mesh. This is exactly what you want, to sleep inside a capsule. You flop onto your back and clasp your hands under your head; you cross your legs at the ankle.

I really like it, you say.

So do I, says Lorraine.

Between seven and eleven each evening the camp is patrolled by nurses on bicycles. They wear white caps and white capes.

Will you two be all right? asks your mother.

Yes, says Lorraine, who will soon be asleep.

They'll be fine, says your father, already impatient. He strikes a match to his cigarette, flicks it away.

Since you arrived in Reception you have unpacked your cases and joined up with the Goldmans and spent an hour in the Amusement Park with Linda and her sister and circled the camp on the Monorail and joined hundreds of others for your Evening Meal, then crowded into the Gaiety Theatre for the 'Welcome to You' Show, and really you ought now to be sleepy. You have had a long day, and there will be another tomorrow.

At Butlin's, there is always another tomorrow.

Night night, then, says Mum.

Night night, you say.

The door clicks shut behind them. In the sunlit evening their shadows bloom and fade on the curtain, and you listen as their footsteps recede down the Chalet Line: your father's black leather Oxfords, your mother's pink kitten heels. They are meeting Auntie Annie and Uncle Sidney at the 'Mix and Mingle Dance' in the Princes Ballroom, where the Stan Clement Sound will be playing. *The Right Beat For Dancing Feet.* Your father has circled this in the programme. It is the only thing he has circled.

Where are you going? asks Lorraine as you slip from your bunk.

Toilet, you say.

The dim-lit chalet smells mildly of mildew, but also of home: Mum's hairspray and perfume, Dad's aftershave, cigarettes. The light-cord in the bathroom makes the same double-click. The bath-taps are identical, the shape of the sink, and here are your face flannels, your toothbrushes and soap. Here is your mother's medicine, her bottle of pills, which you must not touch. They are for her nerves.

Satisfied, you switch out the light and stand at the end of their three-quarter-sized bed.

While you are on holiday your parents will be sleeping together, just as they used to. Your father's pyjamas are folded on top of his pillow, your mother's 'shortie' nightdress on hers. You are wearing brown-and-blue striped pyjamas, bought new from the catalogue. They look exactly like a man's, exactly like your father's.

I wish this could be our house forever, you say.

Me too, says your sister.

At home you must burrow under the bedclothes to find your own private world, your knees tenting the bedding as you take off into fantasies in which you are piloting a craft such as those featured in the supermarionation series you watch on TV – *Stingray, Thunderbirds, Captain Scarlet and The Mysterons* – whose futurism is as familiar to you as the landscape of your home town.

But here at Butlin's you have the enclosure of the lower bunk and need not even close your eyes to enter into a reverie in which you have dominion over a secret underground world and are as powerful and wise as Jeff Tracy, millionaire supremo of

carpet of lawn and rose beds and saplings in regimented rows
that lies adjacent to Chalet Line C – which is where you have
your temporary home – a frizbee gliding perhaps through the soft
summer haze of mid-afternoon, the Big Wheel turning so sedately
in the Amusement Park, and the sunlight gleaming on the roofs
of the cars in the Car Park as you skirt the Sunbathing Lawn
on the periphery of the camp and cruise towards the Outdoor
Swimming Pool, with its splashing fountain, screaming children,
sparkling water and chlorine-scented air, the gaily-painted parade
of buildings on your left including the Tower Building, where the
clock-face is flanked by two chocolate-box soldiers in red tunics
and blue breeches and the legend reads OUR TRUE INTENT
IS ALL FOR YOUR DELIGHT, while beneath you the
Children's Playground becomes the Roller Skating Rink, which
becomes the Putting Green, and finally you turn into the long
avenue between the Empress Building and the Queens Building
and see the cages of the Chairlift passing overhead – the pylons
so stark against the blue sky – and another, older train trundles
underneath yours, the Puffing Billy chugging along on its black
pneumatic wheels, each of its red-roofed carriages bearing the
calligraphic BB of Billy Butlin and everyone so jolly – the grans
and grandads, mums and dads and their children – and there is
Uncle Boko in his bowtie and trademark fez, standing outside the
Tyrolean façade of the Accommodation Office, shielding his eyes
and waving so heartily. And of course you wave back – everyone
waves – which is when you will wake on this first evening to find
your chalet in darkness and your parents tussling in their three-
quarter-sized bed, your mother's voice urgently whispering: Leave

me alone, Joe. No, I don't want to. Please, Joe. I don't want you to. No!

You will retain just two photographs from this fortnight in August, 1969.

The first preserves you and your party in the Lincoln Dining Hall, second sitting for the Evening Meal. As selective as any memory, it cannot reveal the scale of the hall, or the clamour of so many voices, so many knives and forks and spoons on plates and bowls, and plates stacking on plates, cups rattling in saucers, so many sunburned people on their holidays. Instead it shows you and the Goldmans at your table by the window, a ruched net curtain behind you, a bed of white roses outside.

Auntie Annie and Uncle Sidney have joined you late, it would seem, and are yet to be served their soup, which is tomato. At the bottom of the frame the photographer has cropped Linda and Samantha just below the fringe of their identical haircuts. You cannot see their faces, but Annie and Sidney are grinning for the camera, evidently glad to have arrived.

Your father stoops over his soup and looks up as if caught unawares, attempting to smile. Here is the sad slope of his eyes, and here are his cigarettes. Your sister has freckles, a stupefied expression, a hank of white bread in her hand. And here are you, looking across at your mother, aware only of her, as she stares fixedly out of the frame, as if wishing herself anywhere else in the world but captured in this photograph.

The second picture is smaller and finds you and Linda standing on the wet shoreline with your red plastic spades, watching as each hole you excavate mysteriously fills with frothing brown seawater. Linda wears a blue swimsuit with a pleated white skirt, streaks of damp sand on her calves. You wear a yellow-and-brown striped tee-shirt, blue shorts and blue sandals. Neither of you faces the camera since you have no interest in what the future may want of this moment, you have no thought for posterity. It must be her father who takes the photo. Afterwards your father will tease you about her.

She isn't my girlfriend, you will insist; she's just a girl who is my friend.

That's what I just said – your girlfriend!

She isn't my girlfriend! you will shout, and then your father will suck on his cigarette, no longer smiling. You must not shout at your father; you must never do that, not even on holiday.

Sun-up and sun-down, Butlin's is a complete holiday land, with acres of ground for acres of pleasure, and there are so many competitions, so many ways to join in, whatever your age or abilities, including the Knobbly Knees Competition for the Lads and the 'Che-Che Girl' Contest to find the Chubby, Charming, most Cheerful Lass; the Mother and Child Contest sponsored by *The Sun* and the 'Miss She' Fashion Contest sponsored by SHE (Britain's gayest, liveliest magazine for women); the 'Miss Pinta' Competition for Young Ladies over the age of fourteen years and the 'Pinta Personality' Competition for Ladies of thirty years and over; the Father and Son Competition sponsored by Bovril Ltd and the 'Trial by Jury' Contest to find the Happiest Married Couple on the Camp This Week, sponsored by Philips

Electrical Ltd, whose Demonstrator may be found in the Camp Shop throughout your stay.

Uncle Sidney says he cannot wait to see the Lovely Legs Competition, and tells Auntie Annie she should go in for the 'Pinta Personality' Contest, since it is sponsored by the National Dairy Council and she has the natural assets. Instead they enter the 'Trial by Jury' Contest and progress as far as the final round, coming third and winning a hair dryer, presented to them on stage by the Philips demonstrator, a man in a pale blue blazer.

Later your father says he forgot to fill in the form, which may be why your mother looks so unhappy, but when you mention the forthcoming Father and Son Competition he doesn't reply, doesn't appear to have heard you.

He is resting on your bunk-bed, smoking a cigarette. For the remainder of your stay this is where he will sleep, while you will be sharing with Mum. A three-quarter-sized bed is too small for them; she cannot get comfortable with your father beside her.

It's sponsored by Bovril, you say. Dad, we might win some Bovril. It puts beef in you.

You show him the page in the programme, and he takes it from you, stubs out his cigarette and sits round.

Your mother is fixing her earrings, watching from the bath-room mirror. Soon it will be dinner time. The door to your chalet is open, the Big Wheel turning sedately. A Monorail passes over Lincoln Green, everyone waving.

You know what I think? he says then, speaking not to you but your mother. This place is too fucking pally. I'll be glad to get back to fucking work.

Will you? she sighs, and picks up her lipstick and leans into the mirror. She closes the bathroom door with her foot.

Worse than the fucking army, he says, and tosses the programme away. It skids across the linoleum, disappears under their bed.

You leave it there. You don't mind; you don't like to join in with things either.

Your holiday in Butlin's lasts a fortnight, and each morning after breakfast your mother and Auntie Annie will set out with you and the girls to enjoy the attractions, the rides and other amusements, while Uncle Sidney and your father go off to play snooker in the Empire Theatre Building, or to place bets on the horse races in the Turf Accountants, or to sit in the Empress Bar to read their newspapers and drink beer, until Uncle Sidney decides that he will come along with you instead, which is better for everyone, since he is so full of good cheer.

He calls your sister Lolly instead of Lorraine and pretends he is going to lick her – Lovely Lolly, yum yum yum – then lumbers after her when she squeals and runs away. He does the same for Samantha, his youngest, who copies your sister and squeals and tries to flee, but Linda stands her ground, refuses even to smile, and is rewarded with a bear-hug and a kiss on top of her head, which finally draws a grin from her, and that is the end of it.

Your mother is Dolly the Dolly Bird, and he tries to kiss and cuddle her, too. Behave yourself, laughs Auntie Annie, and shoves him away from her. She uses both hands. Your mother's eyes are shining.

As a boy you are spared such games, but should Uncle Sidney notice you watching, helplessly grinning, he will present you with the face of boss-eyed surprise that always sets you to giggling. Sometimes he will wink at you, and you will attempt to wink back. Of course you will wish that he could be your father. Perhaps your mother wishes this too.

Linda is two months older than you are, an inch or so taller, and most afternoons you will slip away with her to explore the camp on your own, since you are both nearly ten, and there are Redcoats everywhere to ensure that you will come to no harm.

Like you, she is unafraid of dares or high places. Seated by your side in your swaying carriage on the Big Wheel, loosely clasping the cross-bar, she will laugh as you crest the top of the arc, the camp spread out beneath you, nothing ahead but blue sky. Sitting opposite you in the Chairlift she will lean over the side and call out rude words to the people strolling down the Chalet Lines. In the Amusement Park you will race to the top of the helter skelter, and descend inches apart on mats inscribed *Butlin's*, almost colliding at the bottom, then setting off again – and again – since the rides are all free, including the carousel and waltzers and dodgems.

All of this you will later recall, and the glimpse of your mother with Uncle Sidney, lying facing each other on the Sunbathing Lawn – entirely alone there, his hand on her arm – and the game of chase that leads you and Linda into the ornamental gardens beyond the Indoor Swimming Pool, where you will lie on top of her in the grass, making manly grunting noises because you are a man, while she makes girly squeals because she is a woman. She is Dolly the Dolly Bird and you are Uncle Sidney, and it is cosy, cuddling up in this way, as you rub your crotch against hers, hypnotised by the tingling sensation in your tummy, your eyes and mouth watering, until at last you become aware that Linda is unmoving, unresponding. She has gone quiet. She does not want you to. No.

Shall we go to the swings? you suggest. It is your last day.

If you like, she shrugs.

You will remember all this, and the silence that descends as you walk towards the Children's Playground, but not the sensation of falling from the slide, or the tarmacadamed ground racing to meet you.

Ignoring the iron steps, you clamber half-way up the chute from the bottom, your hands gripping the sides, your plimsoled feet braced against the rim. Monkey man! you laugh, and wait for Linda to climb the steps to the top of the chute in her yellow cardigan and shorts, then sit with her legs straight out before her. Your limbs and body form a tunnel that she must slide through.

Ready? you call, and she lies on her back as she sets off, her hands flat to her shoulders, scrunching her eyes. She flashes beneath you. She laughs when she reaches the bottom.

Another one! she shouts, and you adjust your grip, brace yourself as she clatters back up. She is your friend again. The chute trembles; your reflection shimmers in the metal. Here I come! she calls, and this time launches herself from a sitting position, her hands upraised, but fails to duck when she ought to. Her arms hit your legs, which causes her head to jolt back to the slide, though this is not why you fall.

You will remember peering down through the tunnel formed by your body as Linda reaches the bottom and stalks from the Playground, holding the back of her head. She is crying. It is your fault, and the next thing you know you too will be walking away from the slide, your blood-streaked palms held in front of your face, blood and saliva drooling onto your tee-shirt.

Where are you going? Dazed as you are, you will understand that you have slipped and landed head-first on the tarmac and this is why the Redcoats are running towards you. One of the men will hold his clean white handkerchief to your forehead, then to your mouth. He will guide you into the First Aid Post, where a nurse will help you into a chair and dab at your face as you moan, your mouth tasting of something metallic, the iodine stinging.

Minutes will pass, then Auntie Annie will push through with Samantha and Lorraine, short buxom Annie with her sunglasses and cleavage, her pale bosoms wobbling. The girls will smell of the pool. Oh my God, Auntie Annie will say; oh my God, and turn aside as your mother and Uncle Sidney arrive at last in their swimsuits, your dark-skinned mother and broad-chested Sidney. His trunks are striped aqua and blue. So too is your mother's bikini. Auntie Annie will not want Sidney to touch her; she will turn away from him. Linda will be watching them.

Only your father will be gone from this scene; he will be back in your chalet, making a start on the packing.

Let me see, your mother will plead, and the nurse and the Redcoat will step to one side so that you can present her with the gash in your forehead, and your fat purpling lip, your two broken teeth. Oh, what have you done? your mother will complain. Oh, why must you spoil things? Every time you must spoil things.

1970

your heart muscle pumping

YOU ARE TEN. Two digits.

It is 1970, the start of a new decade, and for your birthday you have been given a new pair of football boots: Gola 'Speedsters' with 13-stud moulded soles and a seamless semi-hard toe for greater kicking precision. They are worn by top players from many league clubs, and your father suggests you wear them first in the bath, which will shrink them to the shape of your feet, though you must remember to wear some football socks, too. Later you will need to stuff the boots with scrunches of newspaper and dry them out by the living room fire, then treat them all over with dubbin. He has given you his old tin of Carr's, since he no longer uses it. The amber-coloured unguent will preserve, soften and condition the leather, which means your boots will be waterproof.

This is the sort of thing that men confide in other men.

Since you started in third year you have been playing right-back for the B-team on pitches almost denuded of grass. None of the junior schools in your town has a changing room, so you must wear your strip beneath your uniform, then get undressed in a corridor, and parade home afterwards in your muddied kit and your school shoes. The mud hardens to a crust on your legs and turns your bathwater so filthy it cannot possibly cleanse you, and cannot be replenished without running the immersion heater for an additional hour, which you are forbidden from doing. You must wipe yourself down with a cold flannel as the water drains darkly away, then use the flannel to sweep the sediment of mud into the plughole.

The B-team's next opposition will be St Christopher's, the Catholic school, and you are yet to decide whether your new boots will be up to the challenge. For now, you are soaking in the bath in your laced-up Gola 'Speedsters'. Periodically an air bubble will escape from one of your boots, or a drip of water will fall from a tap. One is a *plip*, the other a *plop*. The electric heater on the ceiling makes a buzzing sound.

Downstairs your parents are arguing.

In your third-year classroom there is a small library from which you are permitted to choose a book when it rains at playtime or dinnertime, and that is where you discovered *Jennings Goes To School*, a discoloured hardback in burgundy boards, its frontispiece depicting a group of boys in grey shorts and grey socks, magenta blazers and caps, including the irrepressible Jennings and his best friend Darbishire, a lobsterous clodpoll.

Aged ten, you are still able to imagine yourself as a boarder at Linbury Court Preparatory School, where there are no girls, and no bullying, and the teachers are known as masters and wear capes and are almost always decent. In *The Trouble With Jennings*, which you have been given for your birthday, Jennings has just caused a frantic hoo-hah by flooding the school bathroom with a home-made snorkel. He left one end in the bath, the other dangling over the side, and capillary action has caused the water to siphon away, ruining the music room ceiling. Mr Wilkins is in a hefty bate about it.

Here you fold the page and carefully drop the book to the side of the bath, then stretch above your head for the cord that turns out the light. Your father shouts something. Exasperated, your mother replies: I have told you and told you!

For a moment or two it is dark. Your eyes adjust; the single bar of the ceiling heater glows brighter and you submerge beneath the cooling water, disturbing the sheath of tepid warmth in which you have been lying for the past half an hour. You sink into yourself, holding your breath, and listen to the sounds of your insides and the pulse in your ears, your heart muscle pumping.

Today you are ten. Double digits. Your football boots are an adult size one, and you are four feet three inches tall, a third-year in Junior School. The cards arrayed on the sideboard downstairs confirm your new numeral, your passage from one stage in your life to the next. Yet always there is the question of what happens between these numbers, and how you are to measure it, or even notice it, since time is forever ticking on, your future becoming your past, its movement imperceptible, as elusive as the instant of falling asleep. Like bathwater, you cannot grasp it. Like the increase in your height, or the shrinking of your football boots, or the creep of the hour hand on the clock in the kitchen, you cannot see it.

You raise your nose above the surface of the water. Your body buoys as you breathe. The light from the heating element gleams on your damp knees and you lie very still, your ears beneath the surface, listening to the amplified sounds of the plumbing, the air entering and leaving your lungs, the ceaseless pounding of the blood in your ears. In a moment you will need to pull the plug and emerge from the bath and take your wet football boots downstairs.

Perhaps then the shouting will stop.

Soon this day will be over, your tenth birthday behind you, after which will commence the year-long wait for your next special day, the next change in your numeral. But for now you don't move. You are lying here in your body, submerged in this bath, hearing your heartbeat, suspended in time. One day in the future this moment will be far behind you, entirely forgotten, unless you remind yourself to remember it, so that your older self may look back at yourself, aged ten, on this first day of the new decade, and see how far you have come, how much you have grown.

You are in 3A, where previously you were in 1 Red and 2 Red. Streaming begins in third year and continues through to the Seniors, and you are in the top stream because you are a bright pupil and a good steady worker. Your grasp of grammar is good, your handwriting is tidy, and your attendance and punctuality are excellent. You were ranked equal-eighteenth in the second year tests.

Natalie Hayes came first out of everyone, and sits at the desk next to yours. Linda Goldman came forty-third, and has been assigned to the B stream. You are glad about both of these things.

Linda no longer speaks to you.

Your teacher in third year is temporary, while Mrs Mulgrew cares for her baby. Soon she will return, but for now you have burly, short-tempered Mr Lynch, who teaches facts, spellings and times-tables by rote, just as they were taught you in first year. Come! he will call, and require you to stand by his side at his desk, close enough that you can smell the tea on his breath. As the other children get on with their work – no conferring! – you spell out a series of words arranged as a list, each word concealed then revealed, becoming progressively harder. He nods when you sound out the long ones correctly. Good lad, he murmurs when you have finished.

Then, You boy! he will call on a different day, and it will be your turn to stand and recite a times-table before the whole class. Should a child falter or make a mistake he will hurl a piece of chalk at them, but you never falter. Should there be chatterers he might aim his blackboard wiper at them, but you are not a chatterer. Nor are you tempted to cheat, as some of your classmates will cheat, by writing your times-tables on the lid of your desk. Mr Lynch has taught you that there is a right way and a wrong way for the spelling of words, as for the incantation of your times-tables, just as there are rules for circulating in the corridors, and for the conduct of games. If you don't abide by the rules you will only invite trouble, and no one thinks much of a cheat. Wherever there are rules, you must learn and uphold them.

Am I understood?

Yes, sir, you say.

Here is an example: one afternoon you observe Keith Coatley drawing on the wall at the bottom of the boys' playground. He has acquired a stub of chalk, and his friends are shielding him from view as he draws a face with only one eye peering over the rim of a toilet bowl, then writes above it CYCLOPS WAS 'ERE, and beneath it FUCK OFF, which is so much of a shock you hear yourself saying, I'm telling.

Cyclops is the name of your sister, the one the boys use to tease her, because of her eye that looks so peculiar.

Keith's friends turn to you, grinning. Keith flicks the chalk at your face. You'd better not, he says.

I'm telling Mr Lynch, you insist.

Keith was once your next-door neighbour, but now lives in one of the new houses on the edge of the estate. He was once your friend, but no longer. He steps nearer. He stands very close, but you refuse to back away from him, because he isn't your friend, and shouldn't have stolen the chalk, or drawn a picture of Lorraine, or written a swearword.

Fuck off, Malteeser, he says.

He is bigger than you are, and you ought to be careful, but when he shoves you in the chest you hurl yourself back at him. Perhaps you land a blow; perhaps he lands one on you. He calls your mother a slag. He says she shags anyone. Then he grabs your hair and thrusts his knee at your face. You take the impact on your forearm, and tug yourself free, and when he comes at you again you manage to kick him hard on his shin. You are in the school

B-team, a full-back, a stopper. He cries out, and you kick his other shin, too. Then you make a run for it. You dodge between the boys hurrying to watch the fight, and the dozens beyond them who haven't yet noticed, and sprint up the steps to the top playground, but the bell is already sounding, and you needn't keep running: no one is following you.

Perhaps Keith is in too much pain; perhaps he and his friends will take their revenge on you at home-time. Your ears are stinging, and you are shaking. All afternoon you continue to shake.

No doubt you were right to speak out, and stand your ground, but now you too have broken a rule, because you must not fight in the playground. It is wrong to kick another boy, even if he is bigger than you are, and breaking a different rule. You cannot report him to Mr Lynch, and now you will need to avoid him in the corridors, the playground, on the journey to and from school.

You may never be safe from Keith Coatley, it seems, but the following day a girl comes into your classroom and delivers a piece of paper to Mr Lynch, who unfolds his spectacles, then raises his eyebrows. You are to go to the headmaster's office at once, and wait outside until you are called to come in. This girl will escort you.

She does not speak. Sick with trepidation and shame, you trail two steps behind her.

It is rare to walk the dimly lit corridors when they are this empty, rarer still to stand outside the headmaster's office, which is situated in a sunny, glass-sided bay beside an arrangement of easy chairs. On other occasions you have seen grown-ups sitting in these chairs, which are conspicuous from the corridor. Only the parents of a child in trouble would need to visit the headmaster, who is called Mr Nokes. But now you are in trouble, and conspicuous, and it is this, as much as your fear of the cane, that makes you so miserable.

All the boys are in awe of the cane, though no one you know has ever received it. The cane is administered and received. These are the words you have heard. The boy must touch his toes and receive six of the best on the seat of his trousers, and he must not cry out, for only a girl would cry out, though girls need not submit to the cane. Girls do not behave badly. Some are chatterboxes, and may even be cheeky, which will require them to stand in the corner of a classroom with their hands on their heads, but that is all.

For now, in the Junior School, that is all.

Mr Nokes opens his door and beckons you in, and you are surprised to find Keith Coatley standing beneath a picture of the queen on the wall. The room is carpeted, and there is a scent of pipe tobacco and furniture polish, a stained teacup in a saucer on the desk. The cane is nowhere to be seen. Your punishment is to be shown Keith's bruises. Look! orders Mr Nokes, and Keith tugs up his trouser legs, revealing a livid blue splotch on each shin.

What do you have to say for yourself, boy?

But you cannot account for it, since you cannot snitch on Keith Coatley, who drew a picture of your sister on a wall, and wrote FUCK OFF beneath it, and called your mother a slag and said she shags anyone. You can only say you are sorry. And then you are crying, which is enough. Keith is permitted to leave, but you must remain a moment longer. You need not worry that Keith will take his revenge; this matter has now been dealt with. He has been warned. But Mr Nokes is gravely disappointed in you, and does not expect to be disappointed again.

Do you understand me, boy?

Yes, sir, you weep.

He sends you back to your classroom. You wipe your eyes and nose on the sleeves of your grey jersey before you go in. The other children will think you have received the cane, and you will allow them to think so – you wince as you sit down – but for many days afterwards you will not be able to look Mr Lynch in the eye, and will not raise your arm to answer his questions.

No doubt you are a grave disappointment to Mr Lynch, too – though not, it turns out, to your father, who returns one afternoon from his shift at the Works with two packets of crisps. He has heard from Uncle Sidney, who heard it from Linda, that you fought an older, bigger boy in the school playground, and won.

Keith Coatley, was it? he asks.

You nod.

Good lad, he says, and ruffles your hair.

You gaze at him, perplexed. You had not realized he was still friendly with Sidney, who isn't really your uncle, just as Annie isn't your auntie. They no longer come to your house. You think you understand why. It seems your father does not.

Oh, for God's sake, says your mother, and disappears to the kitchen.

Mrs Mulgrew returns in the spring. She is the youngest teacher in your school, and arrived as Miss Robinson from the island of Islay two summers ago, her accent lilting, her manner patient and kindly.

During her first year she got married to Roger (33), a metallurgist in the Research and Technical Development Centre in the Works. Their wedding photograph appeared in the Leader & Telegraph, and is now preserved between the pages of your Blue Peter annual. You have kissed it, despite the presence of her husband beside her.

Mrs Mulgrew lives with Roger in Mattishall Crescent on the edge of your estate, in a house that is newer than yours, the upper half faced with cedar boarding, a sycamore tree in the garden. The area is called The Shrubberies, but is known as The Snobberies. Sometimes you walk through there. Sometimes you see her. But though she is kindly, and young – as young as your mother – she is also a woman, who became Mrs Mulgrew by marrying a man, and became a mother by having sexual intercourse with him. Sexual intercourse is the same thing as shagging, which is the same thing as fucking.

You dare not speak to her outside of school. Whenever you see her, you pretend that you haven't.

In Mrs Mulgrew's classroom there are no displays of ill temper. Nothing is thrown at the children, nothing learned by repetition. She plays LPs of orchestral music, and invites her pupils to let their minds wander, then write down where they have been. She teaches the succession of kings and queens by creating a mural, with portraits drawn by the children and lines of coloured wool connecting the Tudors, the Stuarts, the Hanovers. And now she has introduced a nature table to her classroom, on which there will soon be some frogspawn, she promises, so that you can observe how the dots in the jelly become tadpoles, then little frogs.

Already your classmates have donated a sheep's skull, a

collection of seashells, a papery fragment of wasps' nest. Natalie Hayes has loaned a glass tank in which there is an arrangement of twigs and a creature disguised as a twig: a stick insect. The first time it moves, the girls nearest the nature table all scream, and several of the boys stand up to look at it.

Of course it came from a pet shop. It isn't from nature, and should not be allowed, but still, you cannot think how you might rival it until Derek Woods brings to school a severed turkey's claw wrapped in a handkerchief. It is two inches long, waxy and bloodless, with a thread of white ligament extending from the end of the leg. If you tug on the ligament it causes the talons to tighten.

Mrs Mulgrew is delighted, and lifts the hem of her skirt to demonstrate how the tendons at the back of her own leg will stiffen and loosen as she raises and lowers her foot. Can you see that, everyone? she asks, and invites the class to stand up. Her shoes are like a girl's, with a T-bar and buckle. Her skirt is a maxi, in orange and brown. This is now the Seventies.

So, let me see you do it, she says, and for the next several minutes, following her lead, you and the other children flex each of your joints, beginning with the ankle and working up to the neck, and it is while you are bending and releasing your knee that you think of your father's two pieces of cartilage, preserved in the Elastoplast tin in his wardrobe.

They came out of his body. They are from nature.

Two days later the B-team is playing Oakleigh Juniors, which means you are able to conceal the Elastoplast tin in the drawstring bag that you use for carrying your boots, your Gola 'Speedsters'. You wear your kit beneath your school clothes, and immediately after assembly you present yourself at Mrs Mulgrew's desk.

Please Miss, you say, and raise your arm as if to answer a question.

She ticks the names on her register, distractedly smiles at you. Yes, what is it, Peter?

I brought this for the nature table, you say, and tug open the lid and agitate the tin to release the wad of yellowing bandage onto her desk. Carefully you uncover your father's two pieces of gristle. My dad had an operation on his knee, you explain; he was injured playing football. These are his cartilages. They came from his knee.

Oh, says Mrs Mulgrew, and gives a little laugh, a shudder of surprise. She leans closer but does not touch them. Her eyes are brown, heavy-lidded; her upper teeth show above her lower lip. She smells of make-up and clean clothes from the washing machine. You notice the pink blotches rising on her neck. Her gaze meets yours. Does he still play football, Peter?

No. He can't any more, because of his injury. And he's old. He can't even run.

Oh that's a shame, she says, and indicates your collar, the red kit showing under your school shirt. But now you're the footballer in the family, she says. He must be very proud of you.

Not really, you shrug; I don't think so.

No?

He doesn't come and watch me. He can't be bothered.

Mrs Mulgrew looks down. She contemplates your offering. Well, she says finally, and folds the bandage over the cartilage.

Thank you for sharing these, Peter. But they are rather private things, aren't they?

Yes, you say.

It's very thoughtful of you to let me have a look at them, she says; but I think . . . perhaps, I shouldn't put them on display. I wouldn't want them to get lost.

She laughs, and touches your arm.

That would be awful, wouldn't it? she says.

You nod. Your eyes are welling, which they must not do.

Will you take care of them, Peter? And say thank you to your father for letting you bring them to school?

He didn't let me, you say, and enclose the bandage in your fist and stuff it back in the tin. He doesn't even know.

Mrs Mulgrew distantly smiles and stands and smooths her hands down her skirt. She takes a piece of chalk to write on the blackboard, and as her classroom begins to quieten you return to your seat and lift the lid on your desk and throw the tin inside it.

What's that? whispers Derek, whose nickname is Woody. He leans over the aisle. Natalie Hayes turns to look at you, too.

Nothing, you say, and concentrate on Mrs Mulgrew as she writes out the date on the board. It is Wednesday 29th April. The year is 1970, and one day in the future you will remember this moment, though you may not want to, and cannot know that you will. For now, you fold your arms and sit up straight and wait for your next lesson to begin.

And then at last there is a dog, a little dog.

It won't stay with you for long. It is a gift for your mother – a mongrel bitch, a surprise – that you and your sister discover on the day of her twenty-ninth birthday. It is whining downstairs; this must be what has woken you. Your parents are still sleeping, and as you come from your bedroom you meet your sister in the half-light of the landing at the top of the stairs. Sounds like a dog, you whisper.

Her left eye gleams. Yes! she exclaims.

You put your finger to your lips, and when you hear another yelp you reach for her hand and lead her downstairs. Sunlight seeps through the blinds in the living room and you look cautiously round. The furniture is arranged as it usually is. Nothing moves. You notice four empty beer cans in the litter bin: Skol. The puppy yelps louder.

The kitchen curtains are drawn, the light softly blue, every sound muted by morning. The electric clock shows twenty to seven. The puppy whimpers, scratching at the shed door, and your sister hurries to greet it. She drops to her knees, opens her arms. The puppy is tiny and furry, jet black except for its paws, which resemble white socks. It licks your sister's face and she giggles, and you notice the wagging stump of its tail and the smell seeping out from the shed. The lino in there is spread with sheets of old newspaper, some of them soaking.

It's done a jobby already! you laugh, but Lorraine is nuzzling the puppy and does not hear you. I'll get it some milk, you say, and empty the last of yesterday's bottle into a bowl. You know where to find things; you are old enough. But the puppy sniffs at the bowl and ignores it. Instead it squats and pees by the cooker. A pale yellow puddle appears on the fading linoleum.

Bad dog! you scold it. Bad dog!

Bad dog! laughs your sister.

Beneath the sink you find an old dishcloth, too stiff and dry to soak up the wet. You throw it back in the cupboard and fetch some more sheets of newspaper while your sister pursues the puppy into the living room, where it sniffs at everything and does another pee, a damp patch beneath the sideboard, which you decide to ignore. It flops onto its side, rolls onto its back, and suddenly comes up again. It sits, then stands, and its tail does not stop wagging.

Come on, you say, come on then!, and it follows you back and forth on the carpet, attempting to snag the hem of your pyjama leg with its tiny sharp teeth. You are giggling now. You are happy, and your sister is too, but still there's the question of where it has come from.

Come on, let's show Mum and Dad, you say, and gather the puppy into your arms. Lorraine leads the way, opens the living room door, scrambles upstairs, and opens the door to your parents' dim, musty bedroom.

What is it? asks your mother, her voice thick with sleep.

A puppy! laughs Lorraine, and you let it fall from your arms to her bed.

No, get it off, get it off me!

Your father stirs.

Joe, what is it?

A dog, he says. What does it look like?

Why is there a dog?

He grins and leans across the gap between their narrow beds. He lifts the puppy on the palm of one hand. Happy birthday, he says.

Take it away, I don't want it!

It's a present, he says.

I don't want it, she complains; take it away from me! Take it away.

Happy fucking birthday, says your father, and lets go of the puppy, drops it onto the floor. It squeals when it lands, and your father rolls back over to sleep, one hairy shoulder exposed. The hairs are wispy and white. After a moment he yanks the bedclothes to cover himself.

Your father has given your mother a puppy for her birthday, and you must help her to look after it. Peter, Lorraine, can you do that?

Yes! says Lorraine.

Don't mind, you reply.

But two weeks later, a wet evening in August, the puppy escapes from your garden. You have let it outside for its toilet, because your mother will strangle it, she swears, if she finds one more mess on her carpet. Tonight she has gone into town with the girls and your father is drinking and smoking in front of the television. It is past Lorraine's bedtime, and possibly yours, but your father does not seem to mind. Perhaps he hasn't yet noticed. Without asking permission you have let the puppy out of the house, and now it has slipped through the gap in the fence to the garden next door, but you are wearing your pyjamas, with nothing on your feet, and you cannot go after it. The rain is torrential.

Bobbie! you call.

The puppy's name is Bobbie, because her paws are like bobby socks. This was your father's idea, the name and the spelling.

Bobbie, come back!

She ignores you, of course; she does not yet know her name, but your father knows, and he hears you.

What's going on?

Bobbie's gone next door, says Lorraine.

The puppy's tail is busily wagging, flickering through the teeming rain as it falls. Your father makes a noise with his tongue, then whistles, but the puppy also ignores him.

It'll come back when it's ready, he says.

She hasn't had her injections, you remind him.

It'll come when it's ready, he repeats.

Daddy, can't you go and rescue her? asks Lorraine.

Come on, let's get you out of this wet, he says, and draws your sister away from the doorstep.

I can put my plimsoles on, you say.

Just come in when you're told, he says, and reaches across for the door. Pearls of rain glisten on the sleeves of his jersey. He turns the key in the lock. Now, *bedtime*, he says.

But what about Bobbie! cries Lorraine.

Don't you worry, he says. She won't stay out there for long.

But Dad! you complain.

'But Dad' nothing, he says. Come on. Move.

You hesitate.

Move! shouts your father, and swipes the back of your head. The blow is sudden, surprising, and is followed by another, but you will not let him see that he has hurt you; you will not start crying, as Lorraine is now crying. Furious, you stamp from the kitchen, through the living room and upstairs to your bedroom.

You slam your door and throw yourself on your bed, and picture the puppy, who will never come back to you, not on her own. She is bound to get lost in the rain.

You are old enough to understand this, and old enough now to suspect that this may be your father's revenge on your mother for not wanting the puppy, and his revenge on the puppy for not being the gift he meant it to be. This may be his punishment of you for letting the puppy outside without asking, and of the puppy for not coming back when he told it to. The puppy ought to have done as he told it to.

Any of these explanations might account for his closing the door on the dog. But whether or not you are aware of them, aged ten and a half, your older self, looking back at yourself, will have no doubt of your fury as you lie on your bed, your face in your pillows, your head throbbing where he has hit you. You are crying, though not because of the puppy – which will surely now perish – but because of this confirmation of your father's inadequacy, his failure ever to be the father you want him to be, that either of you want him to be.

1971

your present becoming your past

THEN YOUR MOTHER has gone. This time she has taken a suitcase.

For several days the island of Malta has been in the news: a man called Dom Mintoff has become the prime minister. You like him, the sound of his name, also the look of him. Here he is on the television, and here in the newspapers that come through your letterbox: his heavy black spectacles, bulbous nose, dark parted hair. Your mother likes him too, though that is not why she has gone back there. She has flown to Malta to say goodbye to her father, who has died of a heart attack, aged seventy-nine, which isn't as old as you hoped he was.

Your mother is twenty-nine and an orphan.

You are eleven, and by now a few more of the facts have become known to you.

At this age you know that your mother was born twelve years after the youngest of her four sisters. That is your aunt Tereza, who sends you cash in a card every Christmas and birthday: two English pound notes. Of her six other siblings, only your uncle Manny also remembers your birthdays: a card but no gift. He is the eldest of her three brothers, and has the same name as your grandfather, since Manny is short for Emmanuel. He signs his cards *From Manny and family*, and you understand he has at least one grown-up son who has a son of his own, both also named Manny. The youngest Manny is the same age as you are.

Your grandfather married your grandmother in 1916. Her name was Assumpta, and she died in the Second World War, though not because of the Germans. She was ill after the birth of your mother, and there were not enough medicines. She died before your mother was one. The eldest of the sisters was twenty-five, and already married with children. She is Marija, who has not spoken to your mother since she married your father, perhaps even before then. Nor have the others, whose names are so hard to remember.

The reasons are complicated, and it does not matter, not any more, since the past is the past; it has gone, and will not be coming back, unlike your mother.

Not long, says your father; she won't be gone long. You'll see.

It seems you have met them, some of these relatives, though you have no memory of that. Among your friends in school, you are the only one to have flown in an aeroplane, since you were taken to Malta when you were three – no older than three – on an adventure you cannot remember but for a scatter of images that may have come from the television, a library book, some postcards.

There is a giant spiked succulent growing against a towering wall, and a donkey leading a two-wheeled carriage into the dark of an alleyway. The sunlight is blinding. You see a group of men sewing nets on a quayside, the sea shimmering blue, a flotilla of boats in the harbour. Nearby stands a group of old women, dressed all in black. Then there's a view of an old city at sunset, and a short, portly man standing beside you, smoking a pipe. He wears a vest. White hairs grow from the tops of his arms. Perhaps he has lifted you up; you cannot be certain. He may be your grandfather. He may be imagined.

You tell your friends the aeroplane had propellers, two on each wing, and the fuselage was silver. The captain came out of his cabin to speak to you personally, the youngest of his passengers. You neglect to mention your sister, who must also have been there, a baby.

Days pass. Your mother's absence continues, and one afternoon you return from school to find your father standing at the living room window, gazing out at your street, as though wondering when she will come back to him. Sunshine glints through the clouds. He is dressed in his new casual shirt and brown trousers, his comfortable shoes. The shirt is easy-care Acrilan, long-sleeved, brown-striped, and clings to the soft mound of his paunch. His shoes are slip-on, and suede. His hair has been dyed again: you thought he had stopped that. He squints through the smoke from his cigarette, then nods. This'll be me, he says.

A car pulls up outside, a dark green Morris Marina. SHEILA

GREGORY. SCHOOL of MOTORING. He looks for his ashtray, stubs out his cigarette. Okay, he says, I'm off.

The Venetian blinds ripple as he slams the front door, and you watch as Sheila Gregory climbs out of her car, exchanges seats with your father. She is younger than he is, and dressed all in blue, a polyester trouser suit. Polyester is fashion's favourite fabric. She talks for a minute or so, then they strap themselves in: *clunk, click*. Your father adjusts his mirrors, starts the engine, puts the car into gear, indicates left, glances over his shoulder, and joltingly draws away from the kerb. Slowly the car proceeds down Bawdeswell Avenue, and slowly takes the curve at the end.

Your sister has gone to play with Deborah Clough. You are alone in the house.

With no purpose in mind you kick off your shoes and wander upstairs and glance in your bedroom, then Lorraine's, and examine your face in the bathroom mirror, and stand for a while on the landing. You consider the attic, but the effort of clambering up would be too great, and you already know what you would find there: rolls of wallpaper, empty suitcases, nothing much older than you are, and nothing to answer the question of what you are looking for.

Instead you stretch out on your father's slim bed. A flurry of rain pitters the window, and you feel a draught seeping in, which must be why he sleeps on this side; your mother would never put up with it. This is her bedroom. Satin-varnished, honey-coloured, the teak veneer furniture contains only her things; the pictures and ornaments are the ones that she likes, as are the colours and fabrics. She is everywhere here, and everywhere absent.

The house is empty. You could do whatever you like, but still you remain on your father's bed, watching the sunlight as it blooms on the furniture, briefly scintillates in the vase on the window-ledge. Time passes, the sunlight recedes, the rain comes again. Each moment melts into the next, and you are comfortable here, your present becoming your past.

At the age of eleven years and six months you have now begun to acquire a sense of the shape and length of a life, and often you imagine looking back on yourself from some far off place in the future, when these days in your life will be gone. But though your older self will know what lies in store for you, and how far you have progressed in your story, you cannot know; how could you know? All things are yet possible. There is your present, and the past you recall, and the past that precedes you, which your mother has now returned to.

You ease round and stand up. The empty clothes-hangers jangle when you open her wardrobe, and you inhale the stale, enclosed smell of her perfume. Your mother loves colour, your father does not. But she has left all her swirly-patterned dresses behind, taking only her dark clothes, the ones that you like, since she is a daughter in mourning; she has gone to Malta to bury her father.

Idly you slide her dresses and tunics and skirts along the brass rail – Crimplene in cerise and buttercup yellow; linen-look rayon in orange and turquoise; stripes and dots and paisley prints in lime green and lemon, raspberry red, budgerigar blue – until you find a small leather case, embossed with her initials, her old ones: D.C. for Dolores Camilleri. It sits among the shoeboxes at the back. The single latch beneath the leather strap is locked, always locked.

You have been here before, felt around in her pockets and handbags, half-heartedly rummaged through the clothes in her drawers. Only now does it occur to you to look again in her jewellery box, which sits on her dressing table. You tip it onto her bed and find among the tangle of bracelets and beads a fine silver chain on which is clustered a crucifix, a medallion of St Christopher, a small silver key.

The suitcase opens with a report, like the noise of a cap-gun.

Still you could not say what you are looking for, if you are looking for anything. Kneeling, your heart oddly pounding, you place the suitcase on the strip of carpet between your parents' two beds. At this age you are well-practised at prying, and methodical. Carefully you remove each item in turn to examine it, then replace it just as you found it, beginning with two thin bundles of greetings cards, each tied with woollen thread, one pink and one blue. *It's a Girl! Congratulations on your Baby Boy!*

Lorraine's pile is larger than yours, since your parents knew so few people when they first came to this town. This was to be their beginning, and yours.

You lift out a small pile of books, around which is wound a string of wooden beads, a rosary. The fattest of the books is a leather-bound bible, and there are two volumes of prayers, illustrated for children, and an old passport, an autograph book, and a tattered paperback called *Every Woman's Manual: A Practical Guide to Marital Relations*. Dog-eared, its spine ripped, the cover says it is recommended by doctors and educators throughout North America. What few pictures it contains are black and white and illustrate the differences between a naked man and a naked woman, and how sexual intercourse is conducted, and the progression of a foetus in the womb, then of a child into adulthood.

But you already know these things. At one time, old enough to be your mother, it seems your mother did not.

The passport gives her married name, though the photograph shows a young woman, not yet your mother. It is stamped 1959 and expired in 1969. Tucked inside at the back is her birth certificate, and yours, and Lorraine's. Your father is named as your father, and you pause for a moment. Inwardly you nod: how could it be otherwise? His occupation is given as *Fitter in Steel Works*. There isn't a space for her occupation, since she is to be his wife and your mother.

You replace the books and take out a bundle of letters and postcards, the elastic band beginning to perish. On one of the envelopes you recognize your father's careful calligraphy. You recognize your aunt Tereza's too, and Manny's, but most of this handwriting is strange to you: evidently there were other people who wanted to share their news with your mother, though not now, not for a long time.

The stamps are Maltese and show the Queen's head, the prices in pennies. Malta was part of the Empire; it belonged to Great Britain. The dates are smudged, but you can make out *1959, 1963, 1964, 1960.* . . .

From the fattest of the envelopes you remove a thick fold of thin paper, the pages densely written, the language peculiar, full of letters you rarely use, in combinations you could not pronounce: *jr, bx, wd, ij, zr.* The words might say anything, and you are glad you can't read them, since you know you should not be here, touching these things. None of this is your business, including the envelope addressed to *Miss D. Camilleri* by your father, which is private.

It is personal, dated May 1958, and of course you cannot help glancing inside it.

He may have been on leave; he must have been missing her. The message at the end is spelled out in tiny red *Xs*, dozens of minuscule kisses, more than half a page of them, the words enclosed in a heart shape.

ALL OF MY LOVE
MY DARLING DOLORES
FOREVER AND
EVER
JOE
X

Your fingers are trembling. Clumsily you roll the rubber band over the bundle and try to imagine him, the grown man who composed this. He would have been forty years old. Forever and ever, he wrote then, before you were born, before the future contained you. All of my love, he declared to your mother, this girl of sixteen, and as you return the bundle to her suitcase you wonder if he still loves her, and if she ever loved him. You wonder if she ever intends to come back to him, his darling Dolores.

You kneel between their separate beds and consider the case, these relics preserved by your mother, and finally – it will have to be the last thing – you tip out a collection of photographs from a pink paper bag, which includes the pictures of your parents from before they were married, and several black and white snapshots of people who might be her siblings, and one that depicts an older man, small and tubby, bandy-legged, in loose high-waisted trousers, an open-necked shirt. This could be your grandfather. His expression is serious, his eyes darkly shadowed.

He is dead now.

The bag smells faintly of strawberry bonbons and also contains half a dozen pictures of your parents on their wedding day, and here again you find your grandfather, standing next to his daughter, a white flower in his lapel. Portly and cheerful, he stands to attention. Your mother's dress is white, and she wears a gauzy white headdress, holds a spray of white flowers. Your father is flanked by another man in uniform, both of them grinning. Your mother alone does not appear to be happy. In each of these photographs, she alone is not smiling.

You stare at the shape of her, at her belly especially; you examine her closely, and confirm what you have always suspected.

The bride was married in a white dress, with her father beside her, and the groom was a soldier, a sergeant. But whatever else these images might wish to present of the time that precedes you, they cannot conceal that you were the cause of their marriage, and all their unhappiness since. Your parents were married because your mother was pregnant.

The lock on her little suitcase is stiff; you must force it to close. The gap between the shoeboxes shows you where it belongs, and how it should be aligned. You tidy the clothes on their rail, and return the key to the jewellery box, and the jewellery box to her dressing table. Then you smooth out the bedclothes, remove any trace of your being here, and as you turn for the door you are stalled by a sadness not simply for your mother and father, or for yourself, but for this moment, which contains their two beds and her honey-coloured furniture, the empty vase on the window-ledge and her lingering scent, the pittering rain and the design in the wallpaper and all the other times you have come into this room, never quite sure what you are searching for.

Perhaps now you have found it.

Quietly you close the door after you and pause at the top of the stairs. Soon you will be starting in Senior School, and this will be the last time that you pry into your mother's belongings. At the age of eleven years and six months, you make this promise to yourself, and to your mother – as if she were still able listen to your thoughts, as if she were still privy to the secrets inside you.

But you are not the only one to be curious about your mother and father; nor are you the only one to be left in the house on your own. Your sister is insistent, tugging your sleeve. Come on, she says; I want to show you something.

Hold on, you say, and place your mug on the carpet, the syrupy dregs of your tea. You fold down the page of your book – *You Only Live Twice* – and allow your sister to lead you away from the settee, through the kitchen and into the shed, where everything smells of detergent.

Since she came back from Malta, your mother has not stopped cleaning. As if it has been decreed by the Corporation – a term of your tenancy – no part of your house has been spared. Everything here has been scoured, everything tidied. Your shoes are lined up in their pairs. Beneath the small, high window stands her Duo-matic twin-tub, on which sits a blue plastic ironing basket, and a packet of Ariel, which washes cleaner because it washes biologically. The sheets, towels and clothes in the basket have been folded, ready for the iron. Across in the corner is the coal cupboard, where no coal has ever been tipped. Instead it contains all the toys you've outgrown: your sister's tricycle and pogo-stick, your red and blue scooter, deflated paddling pool, roller-skates. You are forever outgrowing yourself. So too is Lorraine.

Look, she whispers.

Hanging from the furthest coat-peg is your father's tartan-lined donkey jacket. Your sister pushes the other coats and jackets aside to show you the right sleeve, which is tucked into the right pocket. She eases this out to reveal a magazine, rolled into a tube and concealed inside the forearm. The magazine is an issue of *Knave*, the world's greatest gallery of glamour, priced at five shillings. The woman on the cover is lying on a bed of straw, displaying her bare back and bottom, and the surprise is not that your father should have brought this into your house, but that your sister should have found it before you.

Let me see, you say, and move aside the ironing basket. You spread open the magazine on top of the washing machine and slowly turn through the pages as your sister stands at your elbow, glancing at the women, looking up at your face. You adopt an interested, appreciative expression.

There are no men in this magazine, no pictures of penises. The women are dressed in corsets, black stockings, white stockings, camisoles, stilettos, cork-soled platform shoes, and they are posing on iron-framed beds, fur rugs, large wicker chairs. They are showing their bare breasts and privates, their sun-lit mounds of pubic hair, but more than these details, it is the faces that hold you. Audrey, Shelagh, Pia, Trudy and Eva. Especially Eva, who looks so much like your mother's friend Nadia and is almost twenty-two and presently living with some other young folk in a spacious town house in London's Muswell Hill. She works as a 'glorified clerk' (her words!) in a West End bookstore. You might want to swing by to browse there.

Will you tell Mum? asks Lorraine.

No, you say, for your mother must not know that you have studied these pictures, or suspect you of snooping elsewhere in the house. Will you?

No, says your sister uncertainly.

You'd better not, Lorraine. It'll just make them argue. Seriously. Mum will go mental again.

Your sister nods, disconsolately stares at the magazine. Do you think he's looking after it for someone else?

Yes, maybe, you say.

She scrunches one side of her face, rubs at her left eye, always her left eye. I'm going upstairs, she says then.

Okay, you say, and follow her through to the living room, where you flop onto the settee. You pick up your book. But the story is now lost to you; the words barely register, since you are so impatient to look again at the women in the magazine. You will go back to them as soon as you can, whenever you are next left alone in the house, drawn by an allure that you cannot yet name, that must belong to your future.

At this age your appetite is constant; it seems you cannot stop eating. Here you are in the kitchen, smelling of sweat and smeared grass, the hours you have spent playing cricket. It is the summer holidays. The breeze through the window is warm; your mother's geraniums are luminous red on the window-ledge. You hear your sister's soft voice. She is lying on her belly in the back garden, Nadia's daughter beside her. They are blowing seeds from a dandelion. Ana is five now, your sister is nine.

You run the cold tap and pour some squash in a beaker, drink it down in one go. Momentarily you feel a chill in your belly, and belch. You kick off your trainers and take a tub of margarine from the fridge, a knife from the drawer. The loaf in the pantry is fresh. You tear open the packaging and take out the end-slice and coat it thickly with margarine.

The time is nearly three o'clock. Through the gap in the door to the living room you can see your mother and Nadia, sitting side by side on the settee, sipping martinis.

This is a new thing. In the weeks since she returned, your mother has rearranged all the furniture, every item in every room, including her bedroom. Many items have been thrown out or given away. Other things have replaced them, including a new sideboard bought on hire purchase from Sewell's, the Largest Complete Home Furnishers in town. She is keeping up with the times. Scandinavian-styled, the sideboard is seven feet long and finished in teak, with soft subtle lines lending tranquility and grace. The sculptured wooden handles provide easy access to masses of hoarding space, which includes a cocktail cabinet whose door opens downwards on extendable arms. The catches are magnetic, and you will break them if you are not careful.

Inside the cabinet are bottles of Cinzano Bianco and Harvey's Bristol Cream, Smirnoff Vodka and Teacher's Scotch Whisky, Warnink's Advocaat, Dubonnet wine, Schwepps bitter lemon. To celebrate the sideboard's arrival, you have been allowed your first taste of alcohol, a yellow, frothy concoction called a snowball, which is sweeter than pop and burns in your chest. You could acquire a taste for it, as your father has acquired a taste for the Teacher's Scotch Whisky. He has replaced the bottle three times already; three times that you've noticed.

Your mother and Nadia stop talking the instant you come through the door.

Hello Peter, says Nadia.

Hello, you say.

Have you been playing football?

Cricket, you say, and show her your palms, stained red from the ball. It's our tea-break.

You are flushed in the face, she says.

You nod; you have no reply.

Nadia grins at your mother. Curvaceous, thick-thighed, she wears heavy mascara, pale lipstick, a short orange skirt, and as you chew on your bread you stare at her legs, the sheen of her nylons. Her hair is dyed blond and parted down the middle, curled up at her shoulders. She is as glamorous as anyone you have seen on the television, as disturbing as any of the women in *Knave*.

Peter, we were talking, your mother says then.

I'm not stopping you.

You are being cheeky, she says. Go and play with Ana and Lorraine.

I'm not a baby, you say; I don't *play*.

Peter!

Okay, you say simply, and return to the kitchen. You open the back door as if to go out, then close it as if you have gone. You wait several moments, and when your mother and Nadia resume their conversation you slide in your socks across the kitchen lino-leum and stand with your ear to the gap in the door. Methodically, quietly, you nibble around the edges of your soft bread as you listen to what they are saying.

Nadia, you gather, has a new boyfriend. But always with Nadia there is a new boyfriend, or something gone wrong with the old one. This boyfriend, she says, is a bit of a big-head. He is a know-it-all, and your mother would not like him. He is only little, she adds, lowering her voice; but he fights me. In bed, he fights me. He is rough with me.

Your mother replies, too quiet to hear.

But I like it! exclaims Nadia; I fight him back. I am bigger!

She laughs, and your mother laughs too.

He satisfies me, confirms Nadia.

You are lucky, says your mother.

For you?

The same, she says. He is suffocating.

What will you do?

What can I do?

Another martini? suggests Nadia.

Another man, sighs your mother, and again they are laughing. Nadia shrieks; she is drunk. You suppose your mother is, too.

What about Sidney? asks Nadia then.

Sometimes, answers your mother. Yes, sometimes, still.

He is satisfying?

He is a man.

You hear your sister approaching along the side of the house, and as she leads Ana into the kitchen, both of them garlanded with daisies, you push the last piece of bread in your mouth and step away from the living room. You assume an innocent expression and casually open the pantry.

Lorraine frowns at you. What's wrong with your face?

You shake your head, your mouth too full to speak, your mind too crowded with pictures of your mother, and Sidney Goldman, and Nadia's legs in her nylons.

You have abandoned your cricket game; you are no longer interested.

It is an afternoon in late July, 1971. You are eleven and a half, soon to start Senior School, and you are good at football and cricket, drawing, writing and climbing. Like your father, you are unafraid of high places, including the electricity sub-station behind Mattishall Crescent, a plain red-brick building without any windows. If you were to scale the drainpipe you would be able to get onto the roof.

Woody Woods dares you, and manfully you consider the task, your hands on your hips. The brackets will provide footholds, and there is just enough space behind the pipe for your fingers.

Okay, you say.

The drainpipe is sturdy, painted dark green, and connects at the top with an iron trough where you can rest your arms and pause for a moment to gather your strength. You dare not look down. A raised rim of brick encloses the roof space, and the next stage is to hoist your leg over the coping stone, then roll onto the concrete and stand and move away from the edge.

You graze your forearm on the coping stone, and clunk your knee as you land, but it is easily done. The roof is flat, almost level with the eaves of the houses around it. A warm breeze blows. A dry leaf skitters into a corner, and you hold your arms out to each side of you and turn slowly around. Brendan O'Neil comes next, and does the same thing. When Woody joins you he yodels.

From here you can see into the Shrubberies, which appears to be drowsing. To the rear and right of the sub-station you look down on potting sheds and flower beds, cold frames and washing lines, a motorcycle under a tarpaulin. Then you notice a woman in a green-and-black swimsuit, kneeling in the shade of a sycamore. The shadow is splotched with sunlight. A small child sits in a paddling pool. The woman is Mrs Mulgrew. She lifts her sunglasses and looks at you steadily. Peter, be careful, she says.

I will, you reply.

No, I think you should come down from there.

I will, you repeat.

The furthest horizon is the one you can see from your living room, the Lingwood Road shops. Only the angles are different. The sub-station is silent. You lie flat with one ear to the warm concrete, listening closely, then stand and approach the ledge at the front. You grip the rim with both hands and straddle the coping, your right leg dangling outside, your left knee on the roof.

You know you could not jump safely from here. Even if you were to hang from the rim by your fingers, then drop to the pavement, you would likely break a leg, perhaps even your neck. The contemplation of this possibility causes a thrill in your tummy; your perineum too. Still gripping the rim you ease yourself upright. You stand as though poised on a tightrope, your arms a few inches out from your sides. Slowly you shuffle around and stand perfectly still, facing the roofline of the houses directly across from you, nursing the tingling sensation in your fingers and toes. The breeze ripples your tee-shirt.

What are you doing? says Brendan.

Malty, you're mental, says Woody.

They are scared now, more scared than you are. But high places don't bother you.

Peter? calls Mrs Mulgrew, her voice seeming far distant.

It's okay, you insist, and lower your gaze to the pavement on the other side of the road, then draw back your eye-line, bring it back over the road, until you can see the paving directly below you. Blurrily you register the toes of your trainers projecting from the edge of the sub-station. You hear the breeze, and the pulse in your ears. You feel your heart muscle pumping. You might so easily tip forwards and fall. You might so easily jump.

Your Fault

Peter, please! calls Mrs Mulgrew; don't do anything silly.

Why would I? you say.

At the steelworks your father climbs chimneys and gasholders, all the high places. So does Uncle Sidney, who isn't really your uncle. Danger does not deter them; jeopardy comes with the job. They work different shifts; one clocks on as the other clocks off. Sometimes, still, your mother shags Sidney Goldman.

How long do you stand there, being your father?

For many years afterwards you will remember this moment, and the urge to tip forwards, to plunge head-first to the pavement as Mrs Mulgrew pleads with you not to. That urge will not leave you, or the sensation of falling, the hard pavement rushing to meet you. Many times it will wake you.

1972

this is how your world is arranged

IT IS 1972 and here you are in your exercise book, describing yourself to yourself, unaware of your older self, who will one day come back here to find you:

I am Peter, known as Malty to my friends, which is short for Malteser, not because you can eat me but because my Mum comes from Malta. I have dark brown hair, brown eyes and olive coloured skin. For distinguishing features I have two small scars, one on my forehead and one on my lip. They are the result of a holiday accident. Two of my front teeth are chipped. I am small for my age which is twelve and a half. The half is important. For passtimes I enjoy reading, especially spy stories like James Bond and school comedies by Anthony Buckeridge. I enjoy football and cricket both of which I play for the school at. I am good at climbing. I have one sister younger than me and no brothers. She used to annoy me but now she's OK. I don't have any pets. We had a puppy but it died of distemper. My favorate thing at school is the four o'clock bell and the worst is everything else. With friends I sometimes act the fool. They say I am mental but I never care what other people say. My ambition is to be a multimillionaire with a fleet of Rolls Royce's. My Dad wants me to be an apprentice in the steelworks but I don't agree. I don't know what my Mum wants. She keeps changing her mind, which is a women's perogative.

The exercise is headed Pen Portrait and dated 12th July 1972, a Wednesday. You have reached the end of your first year in Seniors, and this is the last thing you will write for Miss Cosby, who will not correct your spelling or give you a mark; she may not even read it. The following pages are blank.

You spend your last session in English composing this report, and when the bell sounds at four o'clock you cap your fountain pen and shove the exercise book in your stiff leather satchel and join the throng of other boys on the dark stairwell. In your recollection, they will all be boys. You won't remember the smell of them, the piping din of so many young voices. You won't recall any girls. Five more hours of sunlight remain in this day and you are impatient to be free of the building so you can get home and get changed and go out again. You are twelve and a half, still small for your age, and constantly active, forever sprinting, chasing and catching.

It is the twelfth of July, a Wednesday, and your mother is

working till five, your father till ten, which means you must let yourself in to your house. There is a small window beside the back door, the metal latch left unhooked, and though the window appears to be closed it could be opened by anyone. The key sits inside on the ledge, just above the height of your head, and you can locate it quite easily. Lorraine would need to stand on the house-brick that is kept by the bin in the garden. But Lorraine is a dawdler. If this were any other day she would not get home before you.

On any other day you would let yourself in to your house and kick off your shoes, tug off your tie. Clammy from running, you would drink a glass of water and pour another, then forage in the fridge and cupboards for food, which you would eat as you climbed the stairs to your bedroom. Perhaps you would sit on your bed while you finished your tea; perhaps you would daydream. Often you daydream. Then you would change into your jeans, your trainers and tee-shirt, and go to the toilet – remember to flush; wash your hands afterwards – and hurry downstairs. You would leave the house by the back door, carrying your cricket bat, your *County Special* cricket ball, and there would be no need to knock on the doors of your friends, since they would be coming out, too. Woody Woods would be bringing his stumps. Brendan O'Neil, who goes to St Xavier's, would be bringing his pair of old pads that you take turns to strap on, one pad for each batsman.

Your older self, remembering this, may come to exaggerate how often it happens, but most days after school you will gather on Seething Green to play cricket, should the weather permit it. This has been the routine since the start of the Ashes, and usually there are enough boys for five or six on each side, sometimes seven or eight. You are the captain of one team, Brendan O'Neil of the other, since you are the best batsman and he is the best bowler.

The games may last until dusk, until it is too dark to see, and in the misty gloom of those warm summer evenings you will find yourself free of your home, your parents, their shouting and silences, and you will not want to stop playing, even as the other boys start drifting away. In your head you are Basil D'Oliveira, Geoffrey Boycott, Dennis Lillie, Keith Stackpole. England are drawing one-all with Australia, and the third test is about to begin at Trent Bridge. You don't mind which side you are on, so long as you can keep sprinting, chasing and catching.

But this afternoon as you hurry from school you encounter a clamour of other children at the school gates and the stirring, cacophonous sound of a fife and drum marching band. A procession of banners and flags blazes by in the sunshine, passing over the heads of the crowd. You recognize the Union Jack, and the flags of Northern Ireland and Scotland, and glimpse the words *Dauntless Few*, but you cannot see what is happening, what this is about. There are too many other children blocking your way, and most are bigger than you, the fifth-formers like adults, like grown women and men, despite their school ties and their blazers.

You press through to the front. A policeman strides by you, followed by two columns of men in bowler hats and white gloves, each sporting an orange sash, not one of them smiling. Across the street a window flashes open and a man in a vest leans out, casually spits in his garden. An elderly woman comes to stand at her front gate, her arms crossly folded.

You count five bands in the parade, two already gone by, three still to come, and they make you think of toy soldiers, except for the men's paunches, thin sloping shoulders, long hair. The third troop is dressed in pale blue livery, white swags of rope slung from their epaulettes, white frogging on their tunics. Marching four abreast, they are led by a line of drummers drilling a tinny *rat-a-tat-tat* on their snares, then a stocky, flush-faced man with a big bass drum on his belly, who skips nimbly left and right, swinging his sticks, ducking and rearing. The fifers are piping a tune that you think you might know, perhaps one that your sister is learning to play on her Pixiano piano, her present from your father last birthday.

But it isn't all men. Ahead of the next band comes a group of women in hats and fancy frocks, dressed as if for a wedding. They at least appear to be cheerful, while the men behind them have an air of annoyance, though you cannot think why since they don't come from your estate, may not even come from your town, and have no reason to come and parade here. The tasselled banner before them reads *Loyal Orange Institution*, which ought to mean more than it does – you are twelve and a half – but doesn't, not yet. History happens elsewhere; it is happening always.

As the next band approaches, you step from the kerb and walk alongside them. The music is rousing; so too is the spectacle, and many people have come out to watch them, many people you recognize. They are clustered on doorsteps, front lawns and street corners, including Brendan O'Neil and one of his brothers, who live at the turn for Bawdeswell Avenue, which is where, laughing, you pretend to be a piper too, lifting your knees and swinging your shoulders, and cannot at first comprehend what has happened to you, how you come to find yourself on your back on the pavement. You are mental, and sometimes act the fool. But you have been pushed to the ground, and kicked, and now one of the pipers is fighting with Jonjo O'Neil, grappling with him on the grass in front of the houses.

Others are rushing to join in, policemen running to stop them. The bands have come to a halt, marching on the spot, still playing. Cymbals are crashing. The drums are much louder. People are shouting. You scramble to your feet with your satchel and look towards Brendan, your friend. You assemble your face as if there were stars and squiggles and exclamation marks encircling your head. But Brendan isn't smiling.

Stupid Orange cunt, he calls you.

Of course this is how your world is arranged; you ought to know that by now, you have no excuses. You support Leeds United; your friends are Chelsea, Man United, Arsenal. Your father smokes Embassy Tipped; other men smoke Player's No.6. Your father has bought a dark blue Ford Escort; Sidney Goldman now drives a red Vauxhall Viva. The sequence of doors in your stretch of the street runs burgundy and green, burgundy and green, and your door is a green one.

There are these differences, and others; they make sense of your life. But in your town, too, there is English and Scottish, since the steelworks was built by a Scottish company, as were the first houses. Several thousands of men came down from Scotland, a few hundred also from Ireland, Wales, the industrial North, in search of work, a new beginning to things. Others came from other countries: Poland, Ukraine, Yugoslavia, Latvia, Estonia. The people in your town came from all over, but mainly they are English and Scottish, and if they are Scottish they must be Protestant or Catholic, which on your estate means Bawdeswell Infants or St Christopher's, Bawdeswell Seniors or St Xavier's.

If the Catholics have a different cast to them, a different accent or smell, this isn't something you've noticed. Whatever distinguishes a Catholic from a Protestant isn't something you can hear or smell or see. It cannot be that they have more children than they can care for. Your own mother has only two children; Mrs McIllaney has only Bernie and Mary. On the question of religion your father has been determined: you were not to be brought up in a faith; you were not to go to a church. And if your mother is different from other women this isn't to be explained by her religion. If she is so exotic, so alluring to other men, that's because she comes from Malta, which explains her complexion, her accent, her temper. And if your father cannot satisfy her, that's not because he is Scottish, or a Protestant. They may have come from different countries and different religions, but that is not why they argue. Their unhappiness does not begin with God and prayers and priests – and nor will it end there.

Today is the twelfth of July, a Wednesday, and the Loyal Orange Institution has chosen to parade through your neighbourhood. Your friend has called you an Orange cunt, and his brother has pushed you to the pavement. There has been a brawl in the street, to the accompaniment of a mock-military band. Any of this might give you cause to remember this day. But for your future self, looking back on these events, it is the next thing to happen that will fix it in your memory; it is the surprise of the immediate future that will make your past memorable.

Shaken by what has occurred, and afraid you might cry, you walk quickly home. The back door is open: today your sister has got in before you. Then you notice your father. He is standing in the kitchen, facing Lorraine, whose expression is fearful.

You dump your satchel on the yellow-topped table. You smell your father's sweat, his Teacher's Scotch Whisky. Why aren't you at work? you ask him.

His eyes are rheumy, his shoulders hunched. A cigarette burns in his cupped hand. He wears an old brown sweater with no shirt underneath. His hair is uncombed and he needs to have a shave. His stubble is white.

Is he wearing his slippers? He seems an inch or two smaller.

Only recently, standing here in this kitchen, exactly as you are now, you said something you shouldn't have. Whatever it was – cheeking your father – the sudden blow to the side of your head caused you to forget it entirely. You fell to the floor by the fridge, and would not get up when he told you to. You curled into yourself, and he grabbed you by your arm and forced you to stand. He pushed you towards the living room, but this time he didn't come after you and didn't hit you again. Once was enough. Your ear throbbed, the side of your face. You were crying. Now it is his turn.

I didn't go in today, he says, and rubs the back of his neck. Your mum and me had things to talk about.

His face reddens, then crumples. His chest convulses.

Your mummy wants me to leave, he manages, his voice pitched higher than normal.

He holds out his arms, and as your sister rushes to embrace him you turn and walk away; you leave him, this man who is your father, and go through to the living room, where everything is just as it was, just as it ought to be. A car passes on the road outside. Sunlight slices through the blinds, making stripes on the wall, while your father sobs in the kitchen. He holds onto your sister, cradles her head to his belly. Her arms are wrapped around him.

As you climb the staircase to your bedroom you ease off your tie. First you loosen the knot, then slip it over your head. You can wear it again tomorrow, without having to retie it. You kick off your shoes – Clarks black leather lace-ups, size 3 – and nudge them under your bed. Your feet smell; you don't mind it. You close the door, then unbutton and unzip your trousers: size 25 waist in charcoal Terylene with patched repairs to both knees. You undo the buttons on your school shirt: size 12 collar in white polyester-cotton; the label says Invicta. You drape these over your white wicker chair. You will wear them tomorrow, too. Then you gather up your jeans and trainers and yesterday's tee-shirt, which are strewn about the floor.

Whether or not Brendan O'Neil will be coming out this evening, you still want to play cricket. You are a boy, and this is your childhood.

It is 1972 and you are twelve and two thirds, still small for your age, and here you are again in your living room, staring out of the window. The day is overcast, grey. How many thousands of times have you gazed out on this scene? How many thousands of times will you remember it?

The pavement remains three and a half slabs wide to the kerb, but there is moss now in the gaps, and cracks in the slabs, which have settled unevenly. The road remains sixteen feet wide to the opposite kerb, but is no longer so black, no longer so empty. Across the street to your left there is an abandoned car, a Mini with a Union Jack roof, its doors and wheels removed, the chassis raised up on bricks. It belongs to the Sixties. Across to your right a line of ten houses leads down to the curve in the road, which once seemed so far in the distance. Lichen now colours the roof slates. The paintwork on the fascias and window frames has started to flake.

You know the names of everyone who lives in those houses, though in time they will disappear from your memory, first their names, then their faces, ten houses of people, ten families, gone. Of course you cannot yet know this.

Yesterday at this time – this time exactly – your father came by in his car. You were standing outside on the pavement, talking to Mrs Duggan, who lives where the Coatleys once lived, in the house next-door to yours. First you recognised the car, slowly rounding the curve, then your father gripping the wheel, his expression impassive, his eyes on the road. Perhaps he did not think you could see him; perhaps he believed he no longer existed. The car continued past you. It proceeded to the end of the street and indicated, turned right and disappeared.

Wasn't that your father just went by? asked Mrs Duggan.

Looked like it, you said.

He can't have seen you.

He saw me, you said.

And now you are waiting to see if he will come by again, if this is a habit. But though several cars come and go in either direction, your father's Ford Escort is not among them. Instead there appears a flat-bed lorry, expelling scuts of exhaust, a couple of men running to keep up with it. They trot across the front lawns and clamp a transparent bag in the mouth of each letter box, then hurry back to the truck for more bags, each of which contains a colouring book, a box of wax crayons, a balloon.

These are the rag-and-bone men. You have seen them many times previously, but as you stand and watch them today you find yourself filled with a sadness that is new to you, that may well be nostalgia.

Even here, on the Bawdeswell estate, the newest of the neighbourhoods in your new town, there was once the clopping of the rag-and-bone man's horse, and the cries that preceded it: *Ennnneeee ol-rag* BONE! He rang a brass bell and the children hurried from their homes to exchange their family's old clothes and worn shoes for a balloon. Sometimes they trailed along with the cart for a street or two further, a horse being such a novelty, its turds an event. The cart was gaily painted. The sun always shone. That too was the Sixties. But the old man in his cap no longer comes. He has been replaced by this truck, and these much younger men in a hurry.

They come and go in a matter of minutes, but tomorrow or the next day they will return for the unclaimed plastic bags, still clamped in the letter boxes. The full bags will be hurled to the back of the truck, which will include the pile of neatly-folded clothes that your mother has emptied from the wardrobe and drawers in your bedroom. They are waiting at the foot of the stairs, behind the front door; they have been there for days.

Your father has taken as much as he needs, leaving the rest, all the trousers and shirts he kept ironed for years and never wore, all the gifts he accepted and never bothered to open, the scarfs and handkerchiefs and ties, the toiletries. And not only these. All the treasures in his wardrobe are still there, exactly as they always were, including his medals, and the bits of cartilage from his knee. These things are now yours; they will always be yours. But your mother's temper is short, her patience is thin, and if he will not come and collect the rest of his clothes, then she will give them away.

And possibly this accounts for your sadness, which isn't nostalgia – or not only nostalgia – but the anticipation of what is to come, a loss that hasn't yet happened; another one.

Of course you are not the only children who must let themselves into their home after school, or cook their own meals. Many others besides you and Lorraine will earn their pocket money by doing odd jobs around the house; you are not alone in fending for yourselves, though you are the only ones so far whose parents have separated. This is what it is called, as if they were ever anything other than separate.

Your father has gone, and in his place you have two goldfish. He won them for you at the fair on Elizabeth Park, where he also bought you each a stick of candy floss, and paid for every ride that you wanted to go on, and stood to one side and waited until you were done, smoking his cigarettes, as if he were on his own, as if unaware that you could see him. Each time the carousel came around, there he remained, oblivious to the noise, the colour and lights, his two children. Poor Daddy. You waved but he didn't respond. Afterwards he asked if you had had a good time, and promised there would be many other such outings.

Your sister is still waiting; she may always be waiting.

The fish are called Eric and Ernie, and for six weeks now they have been swimming dismally about in a bowl on the kitchen window ledge, the water slowly greening, threaded with faeces. Several times daily Lorraine will insist on sprinkling more feed on the surface, hoping to see the fish rise through the murk to peck at the flakes. It is worth 1p in pocket money to feed them, only 3p to clean them. Round and about they go, their mouths pulsing open and closed, until eventually you will have no choice but to catch them in your hands so the bowl can be emptied and the water replenished. They are slippery. The old water is filthy. But this morning there is no need to chase them. They are dead, floating just under the surface, a cottony floss round their gills. It is your fault; you should have got to them sooner.

You call out to Lorraine, who is sitting in the living room, reading a book from the library.

Look, you say.

She comes through. She covers her mouth with both hands. Tears well in her eyes, spill onto her cheeks, and she looks at you; she waits for you to tell her what to do.

Shall we bury them?

She nods.

You look around for your mother's slotted spoon since you cannot bear to touch them, these dead things. There is a box of Kleenex Mansize on the table. You scoop the fish from the water and lay them on a bed of three tissues and carefully wrap them. You carry them into the garden, and your sister brings the spoon, which she uses to excavate a small grave beneath the living room window. Mr Farrell appears at his back bedroom window in his braces and vest, dolefully watching you. Peggy stands from her alpine rock garden, a trowel in one hand, a cigarette in the other. She wears a headscarf, eye-liner and lipstick. She comes nearer the fence but does not speak to you. A scent of honeysuckle drifts over the gardens. The air is gauzy, as if it might rain. Lorraine sniffs, and smears her nose on her sleeve as you commit your damp parcel to the damp earth.

Do you want to make a cross? you whisper. We can find some lolly sticks.

Your sister shakes her head. Not really, she says. Then: I'm going up to my room now.

Okay, you say.

The spoon is caked in mud, and the bowl will also need to be washed, but the Sqezy bottle in the kitchen is empty. It is a Sunday; the shops will be closed. Your mother is still lying in bed; she was working last night, waitressing at the Civic, since how else is she to afford the food you eat, the clothes you wear, your constant asking for things? It is your job to take her a coffee in the morning, but the coffee has also run out. The milk in the fridge has gone off. There is mould on the last few slices of bread.

You tip the dirty water from the fishbowl into the sink. Outside it has started to rain, and you grip the rim of the sink to stop the floor tilting. You fear you might fall over. You don't know what is wrong with you. Nothing is quite how it ought to be. Then you find that you are sobbing, and you don't know how to stop yourself. You hear the sounds you are making. You hear other noises upstairs, footsteps on the staircase, someone approaching. Then your sister comes back into the kitchen. She opens her arms for you.

1973

you are still a child

THE MOBILE SHOP is old and bulbous, its sides heavily dented, repaired and repainted the same green as the transporter in *Thunderbirds*, whose number you say you can't now remember.

This must be a Saturday, since Natalie Hayes is helping out on the van. She has a job working alongside Mrs Collins, whose husband sits at the wheel and sounds a klaxon to announce their arrival. Natalie is wearing a beige nylon shop coat, seemingly still creased from the box, and you are standing outside on the pavement, furtively watching her. Your heart is pounding, as if you have run several streets to be here.

The kerb-side is littered with scuffling leaves, the air tainted with wood-smoke, a sweet smell of apples. It must then be autumn; let's settle on that. It is late September, 1973, which means you are now thirteen years old – thirteen and three quarters.

The entrance to the van is via the rear – a narrow door and three metal steps – and from inside there descends a smell of fresh produce: sacks of potatoes still dusty with soil and strings of onions, fat leafy cabbages, nets of carrots, bunches of browning bananas on hooks. Lit by bare bulbs, the wooden shelves down both sides are stacked with familiar packets and tins, foodstuffs and cleaning things, but there is nothing that requires a refrigerator, and no cigarettes or alcohol. This may be the last year that the van will tour your estate: everyone complains about the prices, which are due to inflation.

Some younger boys have mounted the steps ahead of you and are crowding the counter, choosing sweets from a glass-fronted cabinet. Loudly they compete to be heard while Mrs Collins serves the housewife behind them. Natalie must attend to the boys, and as she waits on them she looks out and sees you, standing with one foot on the first step. Privately she smiles at you. She waggles her fingers, a small wave. You wave back and look down. The sunshine is sharp, illuminating the dark pitted surface of the rear of the van.

At school when you blush the other boys will lick the tip of one finger and make a sizzling sound, as if your cheeks are too hot to touch. Malty's doing a beamer! But there is no one here to notice or make fun of you, and when your turn comes to climb the steps you ponder a moment, then ask for half a dozen eggs, though in fact you had intended to buy a selection of sweets, just like the children before you.

Six eggs is forty-two pence, please.

You pass over a fifty pence coin and Natalie touches your palm as she gives you your change. Her eyes are green. Her fingertips are warm. You might be two adults – this might be a grown-up transaction – except that Mrs Collins is watching over you, smiling, and again you find you are blushing.

Bye, Peter, calls Natalie.

Bye! you reply, not daring to look back at her, and though your voice is too loud, and lets out a small squeak, for the rest of that afternoon you feel as if you are an inch or two taller, no longer so small for your age, perhaps no longer even a boy, but have acquired some special knowledge that will hasten you into your future.

As if you have been gifted a secret that your mother and sister are unable to share, you speak to them more kindly – more kindly than you have done for days – and when tea-time approaches you stretch out your arms and affect to yawn and ask if they fancy a fry-up, which is something your father might say, if he were still with you. You know how to cook it.

Your mother combs her fingers back through her hair and looks to the clock. Okay, she says; thank you, but I have to get ready. I am going out tonight.

She smiles, and attempts to touch the side of your face, but you step away from her. Your body, which once belonged to Mummy as well as to you, is now yours alone. If you can, you avoid her. You don't like her to touch you.

Will you do some for Lorraine?

Yes, I just said.

Eggs and bacon?

Yes.

Make sure you keep the gas low or the whites will get burnt.

I know that, you say.

And soak the frying pan afterwards.

I'm going to.

Also, use the old eggs before you start on these fresh ones.

I will, you promise, though you have no such intention. Your mother is going out for the evening – you will not ask her where, or who she is going with – and while she is gone from the house you will do as you please.

You will use the eggs that you purchased from Natalie, and in your imagination you will be cooking not for your sister but for Natalie Hayes, who will remain in your thoughts all through that evening, attentively listening as you describe yourself to her, gently holding your hand. She will kiss you; her lips will touch yours. And when later you lock yourself into the bathroom it will be Natalie's face that you see – her dark lashes and luminous eyes, the freckles on the bridge of her nose – as you lie back in the water and close your hand round your penis, which is once again stiffening; these days it stiffens at anything. You are thirteen and three quarters.

Of course you have known how to pleasure yourself since you were nine, but while you no longer require the assistance of a pole or a lamppost, and would never again do it in public, your technique remains little altered; your method is much as it was, and though you will often make use of the edge of your mattress in bed, lately too you have found that you can clamp your left wrist between your thighs while rubbing the flat of your right hand against the underside of your penis. This approach is also effective – the sensation, when it arrives, is equally pleasurable, and just as prolonged – but such knowledge, it seems, circulates separately in your mind from any other information you may have acquired, whether in the school playground or your weekly biology lessons, in the magazines your father brought home from the Works or the paperback your mother once kept in her wardrobe.

In Biology, for instance, you have achieved an A-minus for knowing that spermatozoa resemble tiny tadpoles and form in the testicles before being released into the vagina by means of the penis, which becomes erect for that purpose. Millions of miniscule sperms swim up the fallopian tubes towards the ovaries, where they fight to fertilize an egg, the ovum, which is transparent and circular and immediately plops in half, and plops again, becoming many separate cells, which become an embryo that grows into a foetus inside the uterus, which is also known as the womb.

This is human reproduction, and is performed by adults and depicted in diagrams, but bears little resemblance to anything you have seen in a magazine or gleaned from the boys in your school, including the smokers who gather most evenings by the Lingwood Road shops or sit among the slides and swings on Seething Green.

For example last Tuesday, as you cycled over the field, Woody Woods called out to you from one of the roundabouts, and for a short while you sat with him and the other boys, your bicycle propped against a climbing frame, the evening descending as mist. The roundabout ticked as it turned. Woody flicked away the end of a cigarette and passed you a centrefold torn from a magazine, a photograph of a vagina, grossly enlarged, while the other boys discussed who they had fingered, and who they would like to, including Natalie Hayes. Such is the conversation of boys as they smoke and spit on the tarmac in a swing-park, hacking up fat globs of snot from the back of their throats.

Pretending indifference, you glanced at the vagina, and the photos on the reverse, then watched with the others as Stephen Stephenson demonstrated how to simulate the sensation of having sexual intercourse, first forming a hole with the forefinger and thumb of one hand, then using his saliva to moisten the hole and the forefinger of his other hand. With his tongue between his lips, he slid his wet forefinger in and out of the wet hole.

Fingering, he announced, then positioned his fist over his groin and frenziedly jerked his pelvis back and forth against his moist hand. Fucking, he added.

Wanking! laughed another boy.

You waited a few minutes longer, and when the conversation came round to drinking and who had been the most drunk you passed the centrefold back to your friend and quietly said, I'll catch you later, as if none of this held any interest for you, being so obvious, being so much the ordinary conversation of boys.

But now as you lie in the bath, the water beginning to cool, you lubricate a hand with your spit, just as Stephen Stephenson did. You form with your fist a moist orifice into which you can insert your penis, and as you experiment with your grip you find your mind slipping from thoughts of Natalie Hayes to the naked forms of the women in your father's magazines, and soon settle on Eva in the issue of *Knave*, who works in a bookstore and looks so much like your mother's friend Nadia, and it is when you start thinking about Nadia – curvaceous, thick-thighed, sitting smiling on the settee in your living room – that you are overtaken by a sudden sensation, almost painful, momentarily deranging, that causes you to buck in the bathwater and release an emission onto your forefinger and thumb. You have ejaculated. It is your first time.

Your heart is thumping. You feel sick. The sperm is like mucus, as clear as the white of an egg, and though there is barely more than a blob of it, you understand that you are looking at millions of spermatozoa, millions of possible babies, all of them wasted. You might be their father. You have destroyed them. What you have done is disgusting.

You wash the goo from your hand in the water, and pull the plug and climb out of the bath. You inhale the smell of your clean towel and think of your mother, and your sister downstairs; you think of Natalie Hayes, and determine that you will never do this again.

You are in love with Natalie Hayes. One day soon you will tell her. Your older self, finally as old as your father – the age at which he died – will remember this and confirm it.

Your father.

Of the eight estates in your new town, yours is the furthest west from the soot and stench of the Works. The prevailing winds blow to the east. No housewife on the Bawdeswell estate need fear for the whiteness of her sheets on a washing day; no mother need be concerned about contaminants in the water or air. The worst of the smells are those that seep in from the countryside, the reek of silage and manure. Come the summer the streets in your neighbourhood will be scented again with the smells of cut grass, warm creosote, wet gravel when it rains.

From your house to the start of the steel-site is almost three miles on a street-plan, yet still you will hear the roar of the blast furnaces at night, gas being discharged from the blow-offs, sudden avalanches of coke, trains chugging to and fro, a constant clanking of metal. All through your childhood you will hear this, and hardly know that you are hearing it.

In the east in the evening the sky will glow with the lights that illuminate the Works, and redden like a sunrise when the furnaces are tapped, the molten iron released.

Visible too in the sky is 'the candle', the tallest and slimmest of the chimney stacks, which will burn day and night through all the years of your childhood. Its orange flame is fired by the excess gas from the coke ovens, not that you know this; not yet. Nor do you yet know that the pure white clouds forming over the Works are the product of the quenching towers, where red-hot coke is shunted straight from the ovens and drenched in water to cool it, or that a second chimney is also constantly lit, burning gas from the furnaces, its blue flame lost in the daylight, its stack too short to be seen from the Bawdeswell.

Should you venture any nearer – to play football on the sloping pitches of Elizabeth Park, let's say – you will come within sight of a dozen other chimneys, some sending up clouds of white steam, some spilling clouds of brown smoke across the brute, familiar forms of the steel-site: the domes and ducts and colossal pipes of the furnaces, the coke oven batteries, hundred-foot cylinders, gas-holders, water towers and vast industrial sheds, all of it black, filthy with grime.

Aged thirteen and three quarters, you are old enough now

to roam wherever you like, both in the town and beyond it, and already you have cycled out to the wide expanse of the reservoir that serves the Works, four miles to the north of the town, with no other purpose in mind than to say that you've been there. You have visited the quarries in the south and east too, where the countryside is scoured clean to the rock, and the rock is piled as mountains of rubble by gargantuan cranes. And you have stood on the road-bridge that passes between the ironstone cottages of the old village and the red-brick houses of the new town, from where you have peered down on the railway sidings and the locomotives tugging trains in and out of the site, conveying fifty-ton ladles of iron and skips piled with coal, oddly-shaped pots of road-building slag, and flat-bed trolleys stacked with shining steel tubes.

The entire site of the Works is two miles in length, more than a mile wide, and besides these sidings and the pyramids beyond them – the mounds of iron ore, limestone and coke waiting to be loaded onto the conveyors that serve the five furnaces – the view from the bridge takes in the lime kilns and slag crushers, the Bessemer plant, oxygen plant and sinter plant, the electric arc furnaces and open hearth furnaces, the teeming bays and soaking pits, the plug mills, tandem mills, hot strip mills and heavy rolling mills, the continuous weld plant, the water treatment plant and the effluent dumps.

It takes in all of these things, and of course you could not identify a single one of them, or describe what goes on there.

Twelve thousand men work in the Works, your father among them, but though he will enter each day by one of the checkpoints along the southern perimeter, and work for eight or twelve hours at a stretch, you never will know where in all those blackened structures he spends his days, or what he might do there. He is a fitter in a maintenance crew. Sometimes he ascends to the top of the gas-holders, the chimneys. This much you know, but as for the nature of the work he performs there, you never will learn about that, because you never will ask him, and he will not think to tell you. Why would he?

It is 1973 and your father is fifty-five years old, your mother thirty-two. She at least is still young, however old she might seem to you. Your father has worked in the Works since before you were born, and no doubt he will remain there until his retirement; you have no cause to think otherwise. Steelmaking is now a nation-alised industry and the employment secure, his wages sufficient. Overtime is plentiful. His job is for life.

But though the men who work in the Works are still able to enjoy the advantages of pleasant, well-planted surroundings and well-built homes with decent-sized gardens, in time your town will emerge as one of the least healthful of places to live in the whole of Great Britain. Male life expectancy is among the lowest in England. Steel-workers are almost as likely as miners to develop lung disease, the consequence of inhaling an atmosphere of dust and fumes laden with toxins: sulphur, lead, iron, cobalt and nickel. Higher than average numbers of men will come to suffer from chronic bronchitis and emphysema; higher than average numbers will develop heart disease, some from the strain of constantly coughing. Many will die from mesothelioma, the eventual outcome of exposure to asbestos. Others will suffer the consequences of their bad habits, the smoking and drinking that are endemic in your town and mean that female life expectancy is also lower than anywhere else in the country. Obesity, diabetes, liver disease, coronary heart disease, stroke and cancers of various kinds: all of these will occur in numbers far exceeding the national average.

Another generation will need to reach retirement age before any of this becomes evident, and in the meantime of course there will be industrial accidents, some of them fatal. Statistically, these too will be significant.

In a steel-making plant there is always this danger, especially for the men who work with heavy machinery, molten metal, super-heated gases; perhaps also for those who work in high places – the gas-holders, the chimneys – if they don't take precautions, if the balance of their mind is disturbed, or they have been drinking too much Teacher's Scotch Whisky.

In a steelworks there are bound to be hazards; they may even seem like temptations, though even for a man whose mind is disturbed or clouded by drink there may yet be time to decide on a different course, a less painful end, which might require him to clock out as usual and take himself home – to the place he must now call his home – and ascend to the top deck of the new multi-storey car park, where there are five bays marked RESERVED in the area behind the lift-shaft and stairwell. There, unobserved, he may redirect the exhaust of his car through the ventilation window on the passenger side of his dark blue Ford Escort, using a length of red plastic flexi-hose pilfered some weeks ago from the Stores at the Works. There may not be a note, no explanation in his careful calligraphy, but he will have given this some thought. He will need to seal the gap in the triangular window with duct tape, also taken from the Stores; he may need to drink a large quantity of whisky beforehand. Then the gas, which is odourless and tasteless, may bring him swiftly to unconsciousness, a painless departure – painless for him, though not of course for your sister, who may yet be the one who must find him, if your older self allows this to happen, if he once again fails to prevent it.

The nearest stop for the number 2 bus is at the end of Yaxley Way – turn right from your house, fork right at the knoll – which is where you stand with Lorraine, leaning back on the street sign, blowing into your cupped hands. The sky is damp, a grey so pale it is almost white. A light comes on in a living room just across your left shoulder and you glimpse a colour TV, the Saturday racing on Grandstand. You turn around to look at it, pressing your belly into the street sign.

Why do we have to go on the bus anyway? your sister complains.

You know why, he's working overtime. He doesn't finish till two.

It's two now. Why can't he come and fetch us?

Maybe he's afraid he'll bump into Mum's new man.

But he's not here.

Not yet, you say.

Sighing, your sister hugs her overnight bag to her duffel coat. She rests her chin on the bag, plumps out her lips. Her cheeks are pink. So too is her hat, which was knitted by Mum. Together she and Lorraine fashioned the white pompom on top; they made

a dozen such pompoms, all different colours, one evening when
Lorraine was upset. Your sister is often upset.

Do you want to go? she asks.

Not really, you say. Then: I'm going to the football first.

You can't! exclaims Lorraine. We have to go straight to Dad's.

I can go to Dad's afterwards.

Your sister warns you in a sing-song: He'll be really sad if it's
only me-e-e-e . . .

Doubt it, you say.

He'll be really annoyed with you, though.

Probably.

You hear the bus approaching and step out to the kerb, raising
your arm. It is one of the old double-deckers, green and cream, and
you get on at the rear and follow your sister to a seat downstairs
at the front. The driver's cabin is concealed behind a concertinaed
leather curtain; you can just see his hand through the gap at the
side, working the levers. The engine clatters, climbs up through
the gears.

Fares please! Any more fares!

The conductor is your favourite, the one with long hair. He
wears a peaked cap tilted back on his head, and a jacket covered
all over in badges, a brown roll-neck jumper beneath it. One of
the badges is for Butlin's: *Skegness 1969.* Lorraine asks for a half to
the town centre, please; you ask for a half to the football ground,
and as your tickets feed from the machine, marbled pink on one
side, inked blue on the other, your sister looks at you crossly: her
mean face. You hold her gaze. You look from her good eye to her
bad eye and smile.

Ay thang yew, says the conductor, in a voice like Arthur Askey's on television, and your sister smiles, too.

Will you really come later? she asks.

Yes, you say, after the football.

Promise?

Yes.

What time?

Tea-time.

When's that?

After the football.

Lorraine thumps you on the arm.

I'll be there at half past five on the dot, you say. Will you carry my bag up for me?

Okay, she sighs, and rubs at the condensation on the window. She stares out at the houses, says nothing for the rest of the journey.

The bus takes twenty minutes to reach the new shopping centre, which is called *The Willows* and is constructed entirely in concrete. You have read about it in the *Leader & Telegraph*. It is a modern and spacious megastructural edifice on five levels whose interlocking decks, ramps, stairways and walkways are designed for ease of pedestrian access to a host of commercial and entertainment facilities, including a twin-screen cinema and bowling alley complex. It has an attractive and modern appearance, but already the fountain in the plaza has had to be drained: the winds that whip through the arcades cause the water to shower onto the shoppers. The cinema hasn't yet opened. It never will open.

In the sodium-lit tunnel of the new bus station you watch as your sister gets off, a vinyl sports bag strapped over each shoulder. You follow her white pompom through the crowd until she reaches the escalator, where tentatively she waves in your direction. You wave back, though you know she won't see you. It is here that you will lose her; perhaps for many years you will lose her.

Smoothly she will ascend to level two, the shopping arcade. From there she will need to take the stairs to your father's flat on level five, where there is a camp bed for you ('just like the army') and a lilo for Lorraine ('just like on holiday') but not enough blankets. The flat is rented from the Corporation and is a box containing four rooms. The long narrow front window looks down on level four, an enclosure of empty offices. The only bedroom faces across the multi-storey car-park and his dark blue Ford Escort to the oldest of the housing estates, the Works a mile in the distance.

The football club that bears the town's name plays in a ground concealed among those houses. The pylons for the floodlights rise above the rooftops. It will take another twenty minutes to get to the ground, and once your sister has disappeared from view you climb upstairs to sit with the smokers.

You have a single cigarette in your pocket, slightly crushed, also three matches. If you smoke the cigarette, it will be your first.

The price of entry for children is ten new pence, and you are still a child. You are not yet fourteen.

The turnstile clunks as you enter. The air smells of soot from the Works. The beams from the floodlights are thick in the mist of mid-afternoon, the tannoy distorted. When *Cum On Feel The Noize* fades away there's a hum, a screech of feedback, then the teams are announced. Every visitor is booed, every home player cheered. A few people laugh. Their voices carry clearly. The attendance is less than two hundred: at half-time you will count them. You may buy a Bovril too, as soon as the shutter rattles up on the serving hatch. It puts beef in you.

For now you make your way behind the nearest goal, an uncovered terrace six levels deep, where you choose a barrier to lean on. An old man in a raincoat and cap takes up a position behind the next barrier, twenty yards further on, two levels down. Every time you have been here, he has stood in that place. Once the game has begun he will start shouting.

Across to your left is the shelter of the main stand, where most of the spectators have gathered, including a cluster of boys, eight or nine of them, dressed in Doc Marten boots, denim jackets, black Crombie coats. They kick the corrugated sides of the enclosure when the teams pour out from the grandstand, and the racket is thrilling; so too is the sight of the teams.

The home players in their white shirts fan towards the far goal; the visitors in red and black stream towards you. A dozen footballs zip across the glowing green surface. The players trap, control and pass, bounce on their toes, swivel their hips. Their thighs gleam with embrocation; you can smell it.

Once, for a single season, your father played here at right-back, which is your position, too. This was before you were born: 1959. You have the evidence of his name in a match-day programme, bought for 5p from a stall on the market. Now, for this season only, your centre-forward is an ex-international for Wales, a boilerman in the Works, who has come out of retirement to help save the club from relegation. His shirt is tucked tightly into his shorts, which he wears higher on his waist than the younger men do. His nose is crooked. According to the *Leader & Telegraph* he can spin on a sixpence, shoot with either foot, and cut it up rough if he has to. The last time you came to a game, a Wednesday evening, he wrapped an arm around an opponent's throat and bent him backwards, using the fingers of one hand to gouge open his eyes. He forced him to look into the floodlights. He might have made him go blind, and the crowd applauded when he was sent off, as though he had just scored a goal. They swore at the referee, and the boys at the back sang 'Who's the bastard in the black?'

This is why you have come here. Also because your father keeps crying.

Soon the game will get started. The players line up in formation. The goalkeeper in front of you touches his crossbar, glances left and right to his posts. You blow on your cold fingertips and smell the cigarette smoke on your breath. You tuck your hands under your arms and watch as the referee raises an arm and lifts his whistle to his lips.

Time pauses. All is expectancy.

And if your older self, looking back at yourself, were to decide to remember no further than this, then whatever might be concealed in your future need not be revealed, and whatever might be about to arrive in your present – unannounced, unanticipated – need never arrive. Your future, which has not yet happened, need never exist, and the question of what will become of you, and of Lorraine, need never be answered.

The year is 1973 and you are thirteen and three quarters and this will have been your childhood, which might have been any boy's childhood. And though your older self will one day attempt to summon as much as there is, changing the names, the details, disguising the people, rearranging the geography, perhaps the chronology, in the hope that this may allow him to retrieve the person he once was – that mind, that body in time – which he will fear has been lost to him, should he decide to take your story no further than this, then what will have happened for him need not happen for you, and what will have happened to your sister need not happen to her.

Lorraine need never arrive at your father's flat on her own, half an hour late because she has been wandering the shops in *The Willows*. She need not shout through his letterbox should he fail to answer the door, and need not sit on his doorstep to wait for him, hugging her overnight bag to her duffel coat, your vinyl bag at her feet. And should the chill of that misty afternoon begin to seep under her coat, she need not go to check that his car is where it ought to be, where it usually is, in the area behind the lift-shaft and stairwell in the multi-storey car-park, and she need not then approach it, or be the one who must discover him, sitting sleeping at the wheel, apparently sleeping, his mouth a little open, the engine still running. And of course she need not decide in that moment that any of this is her fault.

Poor Daddy.

Poor Lorraine.

All of these things are yet possible; they may be inevitable, but for now the time is three o'clock on a Saturday afternoon in early

October, 1973, and you are still a child. Your father has not yet been discovered, your sister has not yet gone to look for him, and nothing has yet come to an end, or need ever now come to an end.

Acknowledgements

THIS BOOK HAS benefitted greatly from the generosity and insight of Richard Beard, Mark Currie, Giles Foden, Georgia Garrett, Emma Healey, Henry Sutton, D. W. Wilson, Naomi Wood and my literary agent Clare Alexander. I am, as ever, above all grateful to Lynne Bryan.

This book has been typeset by
SALT PUBLISHING LIMITED
using Neacademia, a font designed by Sergei Egorov
for the Rosetta Type Foundry in the Czech Republic. It
is manufactured using Holmen Book Cream 70gsm, a
Forest Stewardship Council™ certified paper from the
Hallsta Paper Mill in Sweden. It was printed and bound
by Clays Limited in Bungay, Suffolk, Great Britain.

CROMER
GREAT BRITAIN
MMXIX